Princess Ponies

A Unicorn Adventure!
An Amazing Rescue
Best Friends Forever!

The Princess Ponies series

A Magical Friend
A Dream Come True
The Special Secret
A Unicorn Adventure!
An Amazing Rescue
Best Friends Forever!
A Special Surprise
A Singing Star

Princess Ponies Bind-up:
A Magical Friend, A Dream Come True,
and *The Special Secret*

Princess Ponies Bind-up:
A Unicorn Adventure!, An Amazing Rescue,
and *Best Friends Forever!*

Princess Ponies

A Unicorn Adventure!

An Amazing Rescue

Best Friends Forever!

CHLOE RYDER

BLOOMSBURY

NEW YORK LONDON OXFORD NEW DELHI SYDNEY

A Unicorn Adventure! first published in Great Britain in 2013 by Bloomsbury Publishing Plc
Published in the United States of America in 2014 by Bloomsbury Children's Books
An Amazing Rescue first published in Great Britain in 2013 by Bloomsbury Publishing Plc
Published in the United States of America in 2015 by Bloomsbury Children's Books
Best Friends Forever! first published in Great Britain in 2014 by Bloomsbury Publishing Plc
Published in the United States of America in 2015 by Bloomsbury Children's Books
Bind-up published in the United States of America in May 2017 by Bloomsbury Children's Books
www.bloomsbury.com

Bloomsbury is a registered trademark of Bloomsbury Publishing Plc

For information about permission to reproduce selections from this book, write to
Permissions, Bloomsbury Children's Books, 1385 Broadway, New York, New York 10018
Bloomsbury books may be purchased for business or promotional use. For information on bulk
purchases please contact Macmillan Corporate and Premium Sales Department at
specialmarkets@macmillan.com

Library of Congress Catalog-in-Publishing Data
for each title is available upon request
A Unicorn Adventure! LCCN: 2013048652
An Amazing Rescue LCCN: 2014005940
Best Friends Forever! LCCN: 2014006140

ISBN 978-1-68119-495-0 (bind-up)

Typeset by Hewer Text UK Ltd., Edinburgh
Printed and bound in the U.S.A. by Berryville Graphics Inc., Berryville, Virginia
2 4 6 8 10 9 7 5 3 1

All papers used by Bloomsbury Publishing, Inc., are natural, recyclable products
made from wood grown in well-managed forests. The manufacturing processes
conform to the environmental regulations of the country of origin.

With special thanks to Julie Sykes

A Unicorn Adventure!
For Iyla, who inspired these adventures

An Amazing Rescue
For Ellsa, intrepid and adventurous

Best Friends Forever!
For Lucy, Jessica, Andrew, and Harry

The Pony

Queen
Moonshine

Princess
Crystal

Princess
Cloud

Princess
Stardust

Princess
Honey

Royal Family

King
Firestar

Prince
Jet

Prince
Comet

Prince
Storm

Chevalia

Early one morning, just before dawn, two ponies stood in an ancient court-yard, looking sadly at a stone wall.

"In all my life this wall has never been empty. I can't believe that the horse-shoes have been taken—and just before Midsummer Day too," said the stallion.

He was a handsome animal—a copper-colored pony, with strong legs and bright eyes, dressed in a royal red sash.

The mare was a dainty yet majestic palomino with a golden coat and a pure white tail that fell to the ground like a waterfall.

She whinnied softly. "We don't have much time to find them all."

With growing sadness the two ponies watched the night fade away and the sun rise. When the first ray of sunlight spread into the courtyard it lit up the wall, showing the imprints where the golden horseshoes should have been hanging.

"Midsummer Day is the longest day of the year," said the stallion quietly. "It's the time when our ancient horse-shoes must renew their magical energy. If the horseshoes are still missing in eight days, then by nightfall on the eighth day, their magic will fade and our beautiful island will be no more."

Sighing heavily, he touched his nose to his queen's.

"Only a miracle can save us now," he said.

The queen dipped her head, the diamonds on her crown sparkling in the early morning light.

"Have faith," she said gently. "I sense that a miracle is coming."

Princess Ponies

A Unicorn Adventure!

Chapter 1

Pippa woke with sunlight warming her face and the sound of singing in her ears. The music reminded her of her big sister, Miranda, who often sang in the mornings. Miranda was mostly out of tune though, unlike the beautiful voices Pippa could hear now. Curious, she got out of bed.

"Stardust, are you awake?"

Princess Stardust's straw blanket was crumpled as if she'd gotten up in a hurry.

A wave of homesickness hit Pippa as she stared around the empty room. Annoying as Miranda was, she missed her— and Mom and her little brother, Jack. Did they miss Pippa too?

Four days ago Pippa and her family had been on a beach vacation when two giant seahorses had taken her to the enchanted island of Chevalia, a world inhabited by talking ponies. Pippa had learned that Chevalia was in terrible danger. The eight golden horseshoes that gave the island life had been stolen from the Whispering Wall, an ancient courtyard wall in Stableside Castle. If the horseshoes weren't hanging back on the wall in time for Midsummer Day, their magical energy couldn't be

renewed by the Midsummer sun and
Chevalia would fade away. To Pippa's
amazement, she had been asked to find
the missing horseshoes. Along with her
new best friend, a royal pony called
Princess Stardust, she'd managed to
find four of them, but Midsummer was
three days away and there were still
four horseshoes to find.

As Pippa got up, she remembered something important—Chevalia
existed in a magical bubble. No time
would pass in her world while she was
on the island, meaning that none of
her family would miss her. Pippa's
homesickness vanished immediately.

She skipped to the window to see
where the singing was coming from.

Princess Stardust's bedroom was in the smallest tower of the castle, topped with a pink flag, and it had a marvelous view. Pippa glanced at the sea sparkling in the distance before looking at the courtyard below.

"It's the Royal Court," she breathed.

All the ponies of the Royal Court were gathered together, with the princesses and princes in the front. Their colorful sashes and jeweled tiaras shimmered in the morning sun. Crystal, Stardust's bossy oldest sister, was conducting the singing with a riding crop, and the music made Pippa want to dance. When she had first arrived on Chevalia, Pippa had been so shy, but now she was starting to feel as if she belonged here and she couldn't wait to join them.

Pippa quickly put on the new outfit that had magically appeared overnight especially for her—a denim skirt, a striped T-shirt, leggings, and a sweat-shirt—then she hurried down the tower's spiral ramp.

"Excuse me," she whispered as she made her way to the front of the court-yard. The royal ponies smiled as they parted to let her through. "Thanks," she said.

Princess Honey was singing next to Stardust, tapping the ground in time to the music with a sparkly pink hoof. She was very pretty, with a shiny, straw-berry chestnut coat, but she couldn't

quite reach the higher notes, and her voice kept squeaking.

"You sound like a rusty stable door," Stardust said, laughing at her.

Honey hung her head.

"Hi, Stardust. Hi, Honey," Pippa whispered, squeezing between them. "What's going on?"

"We're rehearsing for the Royal Concert," Stardust replied. "We always hold it on Midsummer Day, to give thanks for Chevalia and the magical horseshoes. But Honey won't be allowed to sing if she keeps on making that racket." She playfully nudged her older sister.

Honey's brown eyes filled with tears. "You're so mean!" she said. Pushing past

Stardust, she trotted out of the court-yard.

"There isn't going to be a concert if we don't find the horseshoes," said Pippa. "But before we start searching for them, you'd better find Honey and say sorry for hurting her feelings."

Stardust was surprised. "I was only teasing. I didn't mean to upset her—I forgot how much she wanted to sing the solo."

Stardust was anxious to make it up to her sister, so together they sneaked out of the Royal Courtyard.

Once outside, she whinnied to Pippa, "Get on my back."

Pippa jumped onto Stardust's snowy white back, and they cantered off to look for Honey.

"There she is," Pippa said, pointing, as they left the castle over the drawbridge.

"She's heading for the Grasslands," Stardust said, galloping after her.

Leaning forward like a racing jockey, Pippa buried her fingers in Stardust's mane. The pony galloped so fast that the air rushed at Pippa's face, making her eyes water and her hair stream out behind her in dark, wavy ribbons.

Honey didn't stop at the Grasslands but galloped on across the Savannah.

"Where's she going?" Pippa shouted.

"I don't know." Stardust sounded worried. "This is the way to the Cloud Forest, but she can't be going there."

"Why not?"

Stardust's stride faltered slightly. "Because it's haunted."

Pippa tightened her fingers on Stardust's mane, knowing that if Honey entered the haunted forest, she and Stardust would have to follow her.

"Faster," Pippa urged.

Stardust lunged forward.

"Honey, wait!" called Pippa. "Stardust has something to say to you."

They were almost at the edge of the Cloud Forest when Stardust finally caught up with Honey.

"I'm sorry," Stardust panted. Her sides were heaving and Pippa slid from her back to give her a chance to catch her breath. "I didn't mean to hurt your feelings."

"I can't sing either," Pippa confided. "I'm useless at it, and I get so shy I blush."

"You, shy!" Stardust and Honey exclaimed together.

Pippa nodded. "I'm very shy about lots of things, but Mom says if you pretend to be confident, then everyone will think you are."

Stardust was impressed. "That's great advice! I never guessed that you were shy about anything."

"So where were you going, Honey?" Pippa asked. "Have you got a secret hideaway?"

Honey blushed and shuffled her hooves. "Sort of," she admitted. "If I tell you the truth, you won't believe me."

"Why won't we believe you?" asked Pippa.

"It's a secret, so you have to promise not to tell anyone," Honey said. "I was going to see my friend Goldie. She lives in the Cloud Forest."

"No one lives in the Cloud Forest," said Stardust.

Honey took a deep breath. "She's a unicorn."

"A unicorn?" Pippa asked, surprised. "Unicorns are real?"

"Oh, please!" Stardust snorted with laughter, until she noticed that Pippa was glaring at her. "There's no such thing as a unicorn," she said. "Unicorns are make-believe—they only exist in bedtime stories for foals. Besides, you wouldn't dare go into the Cloud Forest—everyone knows it's haunted."

Just then a beautiful noise drifted toward them. As they stood and listened, Pippa wished her ears could prick up to detect sounds like Stardust's and Honey's.

"What's that?" she whispered.

"It's the ghosts!" neighed Stardust. "Hop on my back, Pippa. We should get out of here."

Now it was Honey's turn to laugh. "Oh, please!" she said. "There's no such thing as a ghost. That's the sound of the unicorns' song."

"It's beautiful," Pippa said, feeling herself soothed as if by a lullaby.

"It's amazing!" said Honey. "But I've never heard them sing together like that. We must find Goldie and see what's happening."

"No!" Stardust dug her hooves into the ground. "You can't go into the Cloud Forest. It's far too scary."

"I'm not scared," Honey said stubbornly.

"Wait!" Pippa said, as Stardust started to trot away. "If most ponies are too afraid to enter the Cloud Forest, doesn't that make it a perfect place to hide a horseshoe?"

Stardust stopped and stared at Pippa. "You're right," she agreed.

"Let's go then," Pippa said bravely. "We can look for horseshoes and singing unicorns at the same time."

Chapter 2

Stardust hesitated, but Pippa and Honey were already stepping toward the line of trees that marked the entrance to the Cloud Forest. A thick mist swirled around the trees, making it impossible to see more than a tail's length ahead. Pippa took tiny steps, squinting to try to see her way.

"Watch out," Honey called, tossing her red-brown mane.

Pippa stopped. A thick green bundle of vines, coarse like old rope, wound down from an enormous tree and blocked their way.

"Are they poisonous?" she asked.

"No, just heavy," Honey said, pushing them back with her nose as Pippa and Stardust joined her. "The first time I came here, the vines took me by surprise and I walked straight into them. You should have seen the bruise I got—it hurt for days."

"They're very easy to miss in this mist," said Pippa.

Pippa walked past the vines, holding them out of the way, then let them go when Stardust and Honey were clear.

"Vines like that could knock out an

elephant," Pippa giggled, watching them swing back across the path like a giant pendulum.

"What's an elephant?" Honey and Stardust asked together.

"Well," Pippa began, searching for the right words. "Elephants are much bigger than ponies, and have thick gray skin. They have long trunks that extend from their faces that they use to drink water."

"Now *that* sounds like a creature for a bedtime story!" said Honey.

"Not if you want a good night's sleep!" Stardust laughed. "They sound scary."

As they walked farther into the forest, the mist closed in behind them and seemed to swallow them up. Pippa stared around nervously, half expecting a dinosaur to lumber out of the over-sized trees. The ground was springy with a thick carpet of leaves. A huge, green plant grew everywhere, with leaves like airplane wings and vibrant red flowers.

"It's like an ancient forest," she whispered.

"It is an ancient forest," Honey whispered back.

"It smells wonderful." Stardust stopped to take a deep breath.

"Listen." Pippa tilted her head to one side. She could still hear voices singing in the distance, but now there was a new, burbling noise competing with them. "What is that?" she asked.

The sound was familiar but she couldn't figure out what it was.

Stardust tossed her head. "I can hear it too."

"It's a stream," said Honey. "The forest has lots of brooks and ponds. They're partly why everything grows so well here."

The ground became spongier as they followed the sound of the beautiful voices. Water oozed through Pippa's sandals, making her toes wet. Stardust daintily flicked her hooves, showering Pippa's legs with sparkling droplets of moisture. Pippa couldn't help giggling. The noise sounded out of place in the impressive forest, like laughing out loud in a library.

"That was cold!" she said.

"Sorry." Stardust hung back so that she didn't splash Pippa anymore.

The ground grew boggier until, finally, they reached a brook. It was small enough to jump. Honey went first, clearing it easily, then turned back and called for the others to join her.

Before Pippa could go anywhere though, something buzzed above her head, producing a breeze that lifted her hair and tickled her neck.

"Eeek!" Stardust whinnied, turning around.

Her eyes were wide with fright and she jumped, her brown hooves pawing at the air.

Pippa's mouth fell open. Dropping down on the leafy ground, she covered her head with her arms. A bird-sized creature darted overhead, red flames shooting from its mouth.

"Help! A dragon!" neighed Stardust.

Honey almost fell over her pink hooves laughing. "A *dragonfly*," she said. "Stand still and stop panicking.

Dragonflies won't hurt you, though accidents can happen if you get in their way."

Pippa's heart beat rapidly. It was all very well for Honey to tell them to stand still, but knowing what to do and actually doing it were two very different things. She slowly stood up and stroked Stardust's trembling neck. Stardust whinnied softly. The dragon-fly circled above them. In a whirl of electric-blue wings, it spun away.

Pippa exhaled in relief. "Wow!"

Chevalia was full of magical surprises. Yesterday she'd met talking horseflies, and now here was this amazing fire-breathing dragonfly. What would she see next?

The music was growing louder. It made Pippa think of tinkling raindrops and colorful rainbows sparkling in the sunshine. She hurried on, eager to discover where it was coming from. The mist began to thin out. In places it hovered around her waist so that she felt like she was swimming through it.

Pippa was so wrapped up in the magical surroundings and the sweet melody of the music that she almost missed the dog crossing the path ahead. It was only when Honey shouted out that she looked up.

"Goldie!" Honey called.

The creature bucked, kicking out its back legs, and Pippa realized it wasn't a dog at all. It looked more like a tiny pony, rose-tinted brown with a flowing blond tail.

Honey took off, galloping after her.

"Wait for us!" shouted Pippa and Stardust.

Pippa's heart hammered against her ribs as they raced into the trees after Honey. What if they lost her? How would they ever find their way back out of the enchanted Cloud Forest? Fallen branches snapped under her feet and damp leaves were kicked up in her face. Pippa pushed herself to run harder, determined not to be left behind.

After a long chase, she and Stardust burst into a small clearing carpeted with mossy flowers, their golden petals shining like the rising sun. Honey stood at the base of a tree, its trunk twisted with age. She was speaking softly to someone, and Pippa looked around to see who it was.

A low branch stretched, like a twiggy arm, from the tree into the clearing. Perched gracefully on the middle of the branch was the strange, rose-tinted brown pony. Its silky tail flowed down like a waterfall. It had soft brown eyes and a blond mane. Pippa couldn't help staring at the creature's forehead. She blinked but it was still there. The creature definitely had a gold spiraled horn in the middle of its forehead. Pippa's breath caught in her throat.

"A real unicorn," she whispered, blinking to check that she wasn't imagining the beautiful creature.

"This is Goldie," Honey said, turning around to face them.

"Hello," Goldie said, her voice like the tinkle of bells.

"Hello," Stardust said, curtsying.

Pippa curtsied on trembling legs.

Her voice stuck in her throat and she couldn't speak. The unicorn was a smaller, more delicate copy of Honey! Not wanting to be caught staring, Pippa lowered her eyes.

"Hello, Stardust. Hello, Pippa," said Goldie. "Honey's just been telling me all about you."

"Hello," Pippa said, finally finding her voice.

The unicorn was much smaller than she had expected—not that Pippa had ever expected to meet a real unicorn. But then she had never expected to meet giant seahorses or talking ponies either. On Chevalia it seemed that just about anything was possible.

Pippa was amazed by the tiny unicorn, her golden horn shining brightly in the patchy light of the forest. Pippa's gaze flicked to Honey. There was no denying it. Honey and Goldie were almost identical.

"I'm so glad you came today," Goldie continued in her sweet, tinkling voice. "Strange things have been happening here in the Cloud Forest. This morning when we sang our waking song, a tree sang back to us."

Honey was puzzled. "A tree sang back to you?" she asked.

Goldie nodded, dipping her head. "The others are still singing to it."

"A singing tree," Pippa wondered aloud. It sounded like magic—the sort of magic that might come from a very special horseshoe. "Where's this tree?" she asked. "Can you take us there?"

Goldie looked uncertain. "I could, but it's in the very heart of the forest. And my family might be surprised to see you—they've never seen a real live girl before. Are you sure you want to make the journey?"

"Yes," said Pippa. Turning to Stardust, she explained her thinking about the magical horseshoe.

Stardust whinnied with excitement. "We must look at this tree!" she exclaimed. "Please, can you take us there?"

Goldie gracefully sprang down from the branch. "Yes, follow me."

Chapter 3

The deeper they went into the Cloud Forest, the scarier it became. Sometimes the mist swirled around them so thickly that it was impossible for Pippa to see her own feet. Shivering a little, she wondered what the royal ponies thought about their sudden departure from singing practice. Would they come looking for them if they failed to return?

The ancient trees were enormous, and branches brushed against her like gigantic spiderwebs. But with Goldie leading the way, her horn shining brightly in the gloom, Pippa's courage came back.

After a while she heard the roar of water. The trees thinned and they came to a huge, raging river of muddy brown water. Goldie stopped on the squishy bank and waited for everyone to catch up.

"We're not going to cross that, are we?" Stardust asked nervously.

"It's quite safe if you know how." Goldie tried to reassure them. "Follow me closely and only put your hooves where I put mine."

Stardust nudged Pippa's arm and asked, "Would you like to ride on my back?"

For a second Pippa was tempted, but it wasn't fair on Stardust to make her carry extra weight. She shook her head. "Thanks, but I don't mind walking."

"This way," Goldie said, moving upstream.

She stopped at a slender tree branch that had fallen into the river. Pippa eyed it carefully. The branch only reached halfway across the river.

"There are stepping-stones from the middle to the other side," Goldie said, easing her concern. She gracefully jumped onto the branch and walked to the middle. "Follow me," she called.

Honey went first, and Stardust made Pippa go next.

"So I can jump in and rescue you if you slip and fall in," she said, smiling.

"What if *you* fall in?" asked Pippa.

"I won't."

"Then I won't either," Pippa said.

She took a deep breath, then stepped onto the tree branch. It was slippery with spray from the river. Pippa hesitated. Then she remembered a PE class she'd had at school in which the teacher had asked them to walk along a low beam in the gym. "Find something to look at straight ahead," the teacher had told them. "Focus on that and don't look down."

With the teacher's words ringing in her ears, Pippa inched her way along the branch until she was balanced over the middle of the river. The next part was even scarier because Goldie was expecting her to step down onto a rock in the river. The water roared past with an angry hiss.

"It's easy," called Honey, who had already reached the other side.

Carefully, Pippa stepped off the branch and onto the first stepping-stone. She wobbled as she landed, but using her arms, she managed to regain her balance. After that it was simple. The stepping-stones were bigger than she'd thought, and she quickly made it to the other side.

"That was fun," Stardust said, jumping onto the bank beside her.

The mist was starting to thin out even more. Pippa stared around her, marveling at the beauty of the ancient woodland and the huge trees soaring above her. As Goldie wove through the forest, the singing grew louder. It rang in Pippa's ears and made her want to dance and skip. Goldie led them on, until she finally reached the biggest tree Pippa had ever seen. It had a tall, redwood trunk that was dented and grooved like a muddy track. Its branches stretched stiffly out with a fan of whispery green leaves. Circling the tree was a herd of tiny unicorns, their golden horns gleaming in the darkness. Their heads were held high and they were singing loudly.

Pippa gulped back tears. The music was so special it made her want to cry.

"Listen," Stardust whinnied softly. "Can you hear that?"

Pippa nodded. "The tree's singing back to the unicorns."

Every line the unicorns sang, the tree sang back to them like an echo.

"Isn't it marvelous?" Stardust's face glowed with excitement.

The unicorns clearly loved it too. They sang on, their voices high and pure.

Squinting, Pippa looked up the huge, red tree trunk. She was sure one of the golden horseshoes must be hidden in the branches, but where was it?

Suddenly she noticed that one of the singing unicorns was watching the ponies curiously. Pippa smiled, and the unicorn snorted and looked away. A few seconds later it looked again. Pippa stood very still. The unicorn stared at her; then, breaking the circle,

it cautiously trotted over. Pippa caught her breath. In the same way that Goldie and Honey were very similar, so were Stardust and this unicorn. The unicorn planted her hooves in the ground, swishing her snow-white tail as she stared up at Stardust.

"You're funny," she said.

"Excuse me?" stammered Stardust.

"Did your horn fall off? You look really silly without it."

Pippa tried not to laugh. That was just the sort of thing that Stardust often blurted out without meaning to. But Stardust wasn't laughing. Hanging her head, she pawed at the ground.

"I don't look silly, do I?" she whispered to Pippa.

"Of course not," Pippa replied.

"I'm sorry," the unicorn said quickly. "My name's Misty and I'm always putting my hoof in it. I didn't mean to hurt your feelings."

But Stardust was too upset to listen and began trotting away.

"Come back," Pippa said, hurrying after her. "Just because you don't look exactly like someone else doesn't mean you're funny or strange. It's not nice to tease others about the way they look, whether they're people, ponies, or unicorns. But I'm sure Misty didn't mean to be unkind. We all do things without thinking about the consequences. You know, like laughing at someone when she doesn't sing very well."

Stardust started to blush. "I understand," she said.

Pippa wrapped her arms around Stardust and gave her a big hug. As she pulled away, she noticed something shining in the branches above her. Pippa squinted at the redwood tree. Was she imagining things or . . . ?

"Stardust," she said, her voice squeaking with excitement, "what do you see up there?"

Stardust looked up to where Pippa was pointing and gasped. "A horseshoe!"

"It's the fifth one," Pippa said happily.

The horseshoe was resting on the edge of a huge, messy nest. It was a long way up. Pippa shivered. She was scared of heights, but she'd been learning to overcome her fear during the hunt for Chevalia's missing horseshoes. The tree looked easy to climb. There were lots of handholds on its rough trunk, and if she stood on Stardust's back, she could easily reach the lowest branch.

"What have you seen?" Misty asked, joining them.

Pippa quickly explained about the missing horseshoes and how the island of Chevalia couldn't survive if they weren't returned to the ancient courtyard wall in time for Midsummer.

"I see," Misty said doubtfully. "But you'll have to be careful."

"Why?" asked Stardust.

"That's not just any old nest. That nest belongs to a dragonfly."

Pippa and Stardust stared at each other in horror.

"What do we do now?" asked Stardust.

"There's only one thing we can do," Pippa said. "We need the horseshoe so I'll have to climb up and get it."

Chapter 4

For once Princess Stardust was at a loss for words.

"That's far too dangerous," she whinnied at last.

"We don't have a choice," Pippa said firmly. "Neither you nor Honey can climb up there."

"Definitely not," Honey agreed, anxiously glancing at her sparkly pink hoof gloss.

Worry lines creased Stardust's snow-white face. "Are you sure you want to do this?"

"Yes," said Pippa. The giant seahorses had brought her to Chevalia to save the island. She was the only human ever to go there. Many of the island ponies had been suspicious of her at first, but now they trusted her and were counting on her—she couldn't let them down.

Misty raised a hoof to show that the unicorns should pause for a moment in their circling of the tree.

Quickly, before her nerves got the better of her and she changed her mind, Pippa waved at Stardust to move closer. The dragonfly nest looked empty. If she was quick, she could grab the horse-shoe before the dragonfly returned.

"Please stand here, under this branch," Pippa said.

Reluctantly, Stardust stepped forward. "You don't have to do this——" she began.

"I do," Pippa said. She made an effort to sound cheerful, and knowing that Stardust was scared for her somehow made her feel braver.

Swinging herself onto the princess pony's back, she carefully stood up on it. Once Pippa had gotten her balance, she was able to reach up and grab the lowest branch of the tree. The rough bark bit into her hands, but Pippa gripped it tightly as she began to climb up the tree trunk. Before long she had

straddled the branch in the same way she would a pony. Relief made her feel light-headed.

"Easy-peasy lemon squeezy," she called down to Stardust.

"Lemon squeezy? Is that something humans drink?" Stardust asked.

"No," Pippa said.

"It must be what those elephants drink," Stardust explained to Honey.

Pippa was too out of breath to explain that it was just a rhyme.

She looked above her. There were only a few more branches to go before she reached the dragonfly nest. She tried to ignore the prickle of fear that was giving her goose bumps. Pulling herself up so that she was standing on the branch, she reached up for the next one. Pippa climbed slowly, checking that each branch could hold her weight before stepping on it. Every time she went higher, she worked out the best places to put her feet before she moved them.

Far below, Stardust and Honey were whinnying encouraging words. And softly in the background, the unicorns sang as they continued to circle the tree. Their lyrical voices gave Pippa courage, and, as the tree echoed their beautiful music, Pippa climbed faster and higher, until she was sitting on the branch directly below the dragonfly's nest. She was out of breath, and, even though she wanted to keep climbing, she made herself sit still until her heartbeat slowed.

"Are you all right?" called Stardust.

"Yes, thanks," Pippa shouted, glancing down at her friend.

Immediately she wished she hadn't looked down. The ground was much farther away than she'd expected. Stardust, Honey, Misty, Goldie, and the circle of unicorns were toy size. No wonder their singing seemed to be fading in comparison to the tree, which was loudly singing back to them. There was a sick feeling in Pippa's stomach, and she became dizzy. Unable to tear her eyes away from the ground, she realized the unicorns were all staring up at her. It was very scary. All at once it hit Pippa that she hadn't asked the unicorn herd's permission to climb their tree, but it was too late to ask now. She wondered if the unicorns realized that it was the horseshoe magic that was making the tree sing back to them. Nervously she wondered what they would say when she removed the horse-shoe and the tree stopped singing.

"Well, I'd better get on with it." Pippa took a deep breath and then sighed. Now that she'd stopped, she'd lost the urge to climb any higher. And she didn't want to climb back down either. She was tempted to just sit there for a little while.

"No—I can do this," she said firmly.

Quickly, before she could change her mind, she reached up for the last branch and pulled herself onto it. The nest, huge and untidy, reminded Pippa of the crows' nests high in the city trees at home. It was filled with four large, green, oval eggs. Pippa saw herself in the shimmering surface of the largest egg. The eggs were beautiful and seemed out of place in the scruffy nest. Pippa's heart lifted as she saw a sparkle of gold.

"The missing horseshoe!"

It was wedged between the largest egg and the side of the nest. When she leaned forward, the horseshoe was just within her reach. Wrapping one arm around the branch, Pippa stretched out her free hand . . . and froze.

"Oh no!" she gasped.

The eggs were moving. She watched in horror as long, jagged cracks ran

across the eggs' smooth shells. The cracks grew and the eggs began to rock, then to split open. A chunk of shell the size of a marble landed on Pippa's hand.

"Ouch!"

The shell was hot! Pippa quickly flicked it away. A long, slim leg emerged from one of the eggs. It was soon followed by a second leg. The legs waved in the air. A loud snap startled Pippa, and she clung tightly to the branch as the egg cracked in two. A round head with two huge eyes looked around in surprise. More legs were appearing from the other eggs. Soon there were four heads and eight startled eyes peering out of the nest. The baby dragonflies kicked away the broken shells and slowly unfolded their delicate, tissue-like wings.

"Oh!" Pippa sighed, mesmerized by their beauty.

Each dragonfly had a different hue to its silvery body and wings. The largest was turquoise, the second largest was red, the third had a purple hue, and the smallest was pink. The colors sparkled in the weak rays of sunlight that had managed to filter through the thick canopy of trees.

Without meaning to, Pippa had leaned forward for a better view. A tiny roar, followed by a jet of orangey-red flames, made her jump back in alarm. Snatching

at some leaves, Pippa stopped herself from falling. Now all four dragonflies were hissing fire. Pippa's nose twitched as she breathed in the sharp smell of smoke. To her left, a cluster of leaves was smoldering.

"Thank goodness for the mist," Pippa said, staring at the blackened leaves. The tree was too damp for it to burst into flames.

Because Pippa had pulled back from the nest, the dragonflies seemed to have forgotten about her and were now competing to see who could produce the longest stream of fire. Slowly Pippa edged closer again. All she had to do was grab the horseshoe while the dragonflies were busy playing. But the nest was too hot and there was no way she could reach the horseshoe without getting scorched. Disappointment almost overwhelmed her. She couldn't go back empty-handed. There had to be a way of getting the horseshoe! Pippa's thoughts were tang-led like knotted string. Below her the unicorns were still singing. She let her thoughts drift as she listened to their music. Suddenly she had it—the solu-tion to her problem! Trembling with excitement, she leaned out of the tree.

"Unicorns," she called down, "please can you sing me a lullaby?"

The unicorns stopped singing and stared up at Pippa with blank faces.

"A lullaby," she called again. "A song for bedtime. Something gentle . . ." She trailed off, feeling unnerved by the unicorns' collective stares.

Then one voice began singing. "*Hush, little dragonfly, stop that fire. Listen to the lullaby and you'll soon tire. Don't breathe flames, close your eyes. Go to sleep, good dragonflies.*"

"That's it, Misty!" Pippa exclaimed in delight.

Misty stopped singing and the tree began to sing back to her in the same soft tone.

"Now everyone join in," called Pippa. "Including you, Honey!"

When the tree finished, Misty started again, and this time Goldie and Stardust joined in. Honey opened her mouth, blushed, and quickly closed it. Stardust nudged her encouragingly. Honey looked uncertain but Stardust kept smiling, until at last, Honey joined in too.

Pippa smiled at her. It was good to see that Honey had overcome her fear of singing in public. The lullaby was making Pippa feel sleepy, but the dragonflies weren't listening. They were having too much fun huffing out streams of fire. Misty, Goldie, Stardust, and Honey sang on.

Pippa joined in with them. *"Hush, little dragonfly, stop that fire. . . ."*

Was it her imagination or were there more voices singing? Snatching a very quick look down, she was thrilled to see that all the unicorns had joined in. Soon their singing and the beautiful echo of the tree began to drown out the roars of the baby dragonflies.

"*Listen to the lullaby and you'll soon tire. . . .*" Pippa sang on.

The flames shooting from the nest were slowing down. The littlest dragonfly was swaying as if she could hardly keep her eyes open. As Pippa watched,

she settled down with her head tucked under a pretty pink wing. The purple-winged dragonfly was next. Yawning sleepily, he lay down and within seconds he was snoring. The red dragonfly's head was nodding. Collapsing in the bottom of the nest, she closed her eyes. Only the turquoise dragonfly was left awake, roaring and spitting out red jets of flame. Suddenly he looked around. He seemed surprised to see he was the only baby who still wanted to play. With an angry snort and one last puff of fire, he snuggled down in the nest.

Instantly Pippa reached for the horseshoe. The dragonfly opened an eye and stared at her.

"Hush," she whispered, staying very still.

The dragonfly flapped his wings half-heartedly. Then he closed his eyes and fell asleep.

Pippa grabbed the horseshoe, wedged it in her pocket, and began the long climb back down the tree.

Chapter 5

As Pippa scrambled back down, Stardust positioned herself under the lowest branch.

"Thank you," said Pippa. It was such a relief to land on Stardust's back and slide safely to the ground.

"You were wonderful," Stardust said, nuzzling her nose against Pippa's neck.

"So were you . . . ," Pippa said, aware that it was now very quiet.

Misty was staring at her accusingly. "What have you done to our tree?" she challenged.

"Um," Pippa said weakly, knowing exactly what Misty meant.

"It's stopped singing! Listen." Misty hummed a bar of the lullaby and waited, her golden horn pointing at the tree as if inviting it to hum back to her.

The tree remained silent.

"You've hurt our tree," said Misty.

"No," Pippa said, pulling the horseshoe out of her pocket. "It's not my fault. You see, it's because of this horseshoe. It's magic—that's what made the tree sing. But the horseshoe doesn't belong here. We have to return it to the ancient Whispering Wall at Stableside

Castle before Midsummer Day or Chevalia will fade away."

"You didn't say that the tree would stop singing," Misty replied.

Behind her, the watching unicorns nodded in agreement.

Misty quickly tossed her head. There was a flash of gold and suddenly she was wearing the horseshoe on her horn. A loud cheer rang out, and the unicorns stomped their hooves.

Pippa stared at her empty hands and gasped.

"Give that back," Stardust said, walking up to Misty. "The horseshoe doesn't belong here."

"It does now. We unicorns love our singing tree. We're keeping the horseshoe."

Pippa didn't want to upset the unicorns, but she knew she had to get the horseshoe back to the Whispering Wall, for their own good and the good of Chevalia. She did some quick thinking, then went and stood between Stardust and Misty.

"Chevalia is your home too, and if you keep the golden horseshoe, then you will lose more than just this tree. The whole Cloud Forest will disappear. That's why you have to give the horseshoe back. But if you love to sing, how about singing with the royal ponies? Your voices are so beautiful, they could learn from you. You wouldn't even have to leave the Cloud Forest," she added quickly, as Misty started to protest. "We could ask the Royal Court to come here."

Misty turned her back on Pippa and spoke to her family in urgent whispers. Pippa strained her ears, trying to figure out what they were saying.

At last, Misty turned to Pippa and said, "They don't believe your story about royal ponies, a castle, and a wall that whispers. It all sounds like make-believe. They want me to keep the golden horseshoe, but if you bring the ponies of the Royal Court here to sing with us, then they would believe you."

Pippa hopped onto Stardust's back.

"We'll bring them here right away," she promised.

Pippa was very glad that Honey was with them—she'd been to the Cloud Forest many times and had a good idea which way to go. But even Honey got lost in the large forest, and twice they had to retrace their hoofsteps.

It was lunchtime when they finally returned to the castle. Pippa's stomach grumbled as they made their way through the packed dining room. The rosy red apples piled in the feeding troughs looked delicious. There was no time to stop for food, though. With Stardust and Honey at her side, she made her way to the top of the room, where Queen Moonshine and King Firestar were eating from their golden trough.

Pippa, Stardust, and Honey curtsied.

"Your Majesties," Pippa began, "we're sorry for interrupting your lunch, but we have something important to ask."

Queen Moonshine pushed aside a large carrot. "Go on, my child," she said.

The dining room fell silent. Pippa's ears burned as she quickly explained in a loud, clear voice what had happened that morning.

When she'd finished, she heard Cinders snort and whisper loudly to her mother, Baroness Divine, "She expects us to believe that?"

Several other ponies added excla-
mations of disbelief. There were whin-
nies of "Make-believe!" and lots of
laughter.

Pippa was angry. "It's true," she said,
turning around to address the dining
room. "Why would I make it up?
Come to the Cloud Forest and see for
yourselves." She paused to stare around
the room. "If you're brave enough,
that is."

The laughter turned to mutters.
Pippa noticed Divine whispering something in Cinders's ear. Cinders nodded,
and then she quietly left the room.

Pippa turned to Stardust. "I'm sorry,"
she began. "I tried my best—"

Someone was banging a hoof for

silence. A hush fell as Baroness Divine stood and addressed the dining room.

"I say we give the girl a chance. Maybe she is telling the truth. And if she isn't, well, maybe it's time she left the island." She stared at Pippa, her square face tilted, her brown eyes challenging.

Pippa stared back. Her heart was thumping so loudly she was amazed that no one else could hear it.

"Thank you, Baroness Divine," she said.

Divine nodded. "If Your Majesties agree, then I suggest we leave for the Cloud Forest immediately. And if the horseshoe isn't there, then Pippa must return to her home."

Pippa opened her mouth to protest

but thought better of it. Divine was challenging her. If she didn't agree to her terms, then Divine would accuse her of making the whole story up. But the story was true, and soon she'd be able to prove it.

"Pippa, are you happy to take us to the Cloud Forest?" asked Queen Moonshine.

"Yes, Your Majesty," Pippa said loudly.

"Then let us depart," said the queen.

At first the royal ponies chatted noisily and there was lots of laughter as they trotted through the Grasslands and the Savannah. But as the Cloud Forest came into view, the procession

slowed and the chatter died away. At
the edge of the forest, Pippa, Stardust,
and Honey waited for everyone else to
catch up.

"Are we really going in?" grumbled
Princess Cloud. "Hasn't the joke gone
far enough?"

"It's not a joke," Pippa said quietly.

Even bossy Princess Crystal's eyes
were round with fear. Her voice cracked
when she asked, "Does *everyone* have to
go in?"

"The unicorns are expecting the
entire Royal Court," Stardust said impa-
tiently. "Anyone who is too scared to
enter can just wait here."

Many of the ponies were scared,
but no one wanted to look like a

coward. When Pippa stepped into the forest, they all followed. The responsibility weighed heavily on Pippa. Would they be able to find their way back to the unicorns? And would Misty honor her promise to return the golden horseshoe when the royal ponies appeared and sang?

Pippa led the procession of ponies through the mist, retracing her steps from the morning's adventure. As the giant tree finally came into sight, Pippa stared up its thick, redwood trunk to the dragonfly nest, from which a fountain of flames could be seen shooting out every now and again. Seeing the tree once more made her appreciate just how high it was, and knowing she had scaled it gave her a burst of courage.

The royal ponies stopped close to the base of the tree to stare openly at the unicorns. The unicorns stared back in silence. It was hard to say which party was most surprised to see the other. The unicorns and ponies had more in common than they realized, and there was no need for them to be afraid of one other. Then Pippa realized something and her mouth fell open. It wasn't just Honey and Goldie, and Stardust and Misty, who looked alike. The ponies all seemed to have a unicorn double, identical in every way except for their horns and sizes.

Nudging Stardust, Pippa whispered, "Look—every pony has a unicorn twin."

Princess Crystal had noticed this too. Soon she was moving around the tree, pairing the ponies up with their unicorn doubles. When everyone had a partner, Crystal and Petal, her unicorn twin, both raised a hoof and began to conduct.

The unicorns sang first, one line at a time, then waited for the ponies to sing back to them. Their voices complemented each other's so beautifully that the sound was even more wonderful than that of the singing tree. Stardust sang to Misty, Honey to Goldie, and Queen Moonshine to a magnificent unicorn with a tall, golden horn. There were even stocky unicorn equivalents of Cinders and Divine.

"That's so beautiful," Pippa said, swallowing a lump in her throat.

As the song ended and the voices faded away, Crystal and Petal bowed to each other.

Queen Moonshine stepped forward, curtsying to her unicorn double, who

was wearing a tiny gold crown decorated with purple daisies.

"I'm Moonshine, Queen of Chevalia," she said. "That was wonderful. We'd be honored if you would join us for the Royal Concert on Midsummer Day."

"I'm Sunrise, Queen of the Cloud Forest." The unicorn's voice tinkled like a mountain stream. "It would be our pleasure to host the concert here in the Cloud Forest."

The sound of hoofbeats jarred in Pippa's ears. Turning quickly, she saw two scruffy ponies darting away through the trees. An icy shiver ran down her spine. The ponies running away were Night Mares!

She called urgently to Misty, "Where's the magical horseshoe?"

"Here," Misty said, pointing her horn to a fallen log. Then she looked confused. "Where's it gone? I definitely left it there."

Pippa noticed Cinders and Divine sharing a smug smile.

"Divine, have you seen the horse-shoe?" asked Pippa.

"No, I'm afraid not," Divine replied. "Are you sure there was a horseshoe here? Or did you just make that up to get attention?"

The watching ponies shifted their hooves as they muttered among themselves.

"It *was* here," Stardust confirmed. "Maybe it fell off the log?"

"No," Pippa said grimly. "I just saw two Night Mares running away through the forest. They must have stolen the horseshoe while we were singing."

"More make-believe." Divine shook her head.

"Quick," cried Stardust. "Jump on my back, Pippa. We have to catch them!"

Pippa jumped onto Stardust's back

and hung on tight to her long white mane as the princess pony galloped after the Night Mares.

Chapter 6

A thick mist enveloped Stardust and Pippa as they raced through the Cloud Forest. Pippa looked around her, ducking frequently to avoid being snagged by low-hanging branches. The Night Mares had a head start but Stardust was fast—and much quicker at turning. She began to gain on them.

"Stop!" shouted Pippa. "Stop, you thieves!"

In the distance Pippa could hear the roar of the river. If Stardust could reach the stepping-stones before the Night Mares, there was a good chance they could get the horseshoe back.

"Faster." She leaned forward, urging Stardust on.

Mud and leaves were kicked up by Stardust's hooves. Her breath came out in snorts and her sides shook as she chased after the Night Mares. They were almost at the riverbank when she finally caught up with them. As she stopped, Pippa leaped from her back and ran toward the biggest of the scruffy ponies, who was carrying the golden horseshoe in its mouth. Its forelegs were in the water but it was hesitating.

"Which stone do I step on first? Lightning, can you remember?"

"Um," Lightning said, stretching out a hoof, then quickly pulling it back. "Are you sure we crossed here, Thunder? The river's very fast-flowing."

"Useless brother! Of course it was here," roared Thunder. "Why did the Mistress pair me with you for such an important mission?"

"Take that back. I'm not useless—I spotted the horseshoe," Lightning said, blocking Thunder's path.

"Get out of the way," Thunder growled, shoving past him.

"No!" Lightning whinnied in fright as he slipped on the muddy bank and fell, taking Thunder down with him.

There was a loud splash as the Night Mares landed in the river. The two brothers struggled to their hooves, their dark manes plastered to their faces. Pippa and Stardust roared with laughter as Thunder and Lightning splashed around. But the current was too strong, and suddenly they lost their balance and were swept away down-stream. Pippa and Stardust stopped laughing then.

"We have to help them," cried Pippa.

"And save the horseshoe," Stardust added.

They hurried along the bank after the Night Mares. Willowy trees grew next to the river, and their long branches trailed in the water.

"Grab the branches!" Pippa called. She didn't want the thieves to escape with the horseshoe, but she certainly didn't want them to drown.

The Night Mares listened to Pippa and swam to the opposite bank, where, grabbing onto the branches, they pulled themselves out of the rushing water.

Pippa and Stardust stopped and stared at them in dismay. Still clinging onto the willowy branches, the Night Mares stood in the shallow water while they regained their breath.

"You can't catch us now," Lightning shouted excitedly.

Pippa heard hooves coming up behind her. Misty dashed past, stopping at the water's edge. She leaned down, dipped her horn in the water, then quickly stood up. Pippa's ears rang with a cracking sound as the river began to freeze over.

"What's happening?" she yelled over the creaks and groans of the water turning to ice.

"It's horn magic," Misty explained. "All unicorns have a magic horn, and they can do one special thing with it. My horn freezes water and melts it again."

Soon the river was a thick slab of smooth ice. The Night Mares were having trouble standing and leaned against each other for support. Thunder tried to climb onto the riverbank and lost his footing. He dropped the horseshoe, and it skidded across the ice into the middle of the frozen river. Each time he tried to go after it, his hooves slid in different directions.

Pippa ran toward the nearest tree. She climbed onto a willowy branch that was threaded with vines.

"Careful," shouted Stardust.

Pippa's heart raced as she grabbed a vine and swung on it like a rope. When she swung out over the river, she reached down for the horseshoe. Her fingers brushed the cold metal, but before she could pick it up, the vine swung her away out of reach. Pippa pushed herself back over the river. Gritting her teeth, she stretched as far as she could. Her fingers touched the horseshoe and curled around it. She quickly snatched it up.

"Hooray!" Stardust and Misty cheered as she swung back to the tree.

Misty dipped her head and touched the frozen river with her horn. With a groan, the ice split down the middle and started to melt. Muttering and

grumbling, the Night Mares waded through the slushy ice, climbed onto the opposite bank, and trotted away, their heads low.

Pippa threw her arms around Stardust and hugged her tight.

"We did it!"

Misty hung back, until Pippa put out an arm and drew her close. They were still hugging when a voice echoed behind them.

"Well done, everyone."

Pippa turned around to see Queen Moonshine leading the ponies and unicorns through the trees toward them.

She nuzzled Pippa's wavy brown hair with her nose. "You've been very brave. We should never have doubted you."

"Stardust and Misty were very brave too," Pippa said quickly.

"Yes, they were," Queen Moonshine agreed. "And now it's time to return to the castle. We must hang this fifth horseshoe back on the wall where it belongs before anything else happens to it." She turned to address the unicorns. "Please, would you all grant me the honor of joining us? We'd love you to stay with us and sing at our special Midsummer concert."

The unicorns shuffled awkwardly, until Misty stepped forward.

"Thank you. That would be a great honor for us too, but . . ." She hesitated. "We're unable to leave the Cloud Forest."

"Why?" Stardust blurted out, unable to hide her disappointment.

Misty still hesitated, blushing. "We've never left the forest before—we're too scared to. We know about the ghosts who live beyond the trees."

Pippa bit the inside of her lip to stop a smile. "We thought there were ghosts in the Cloud Forest until we met you, but there's no such thing." She pushed a damp curl out of her face. "And even if you are scared, you shouldn't let it stop you from doing the things you want. I was terrified when I climbed the tree and faced the baby dragonflies. Honey was scared when we all sang the lullaby together. The royal ponies were frightened to come into the Cloud Forest. But we all managed to conquer our fears."

"Please come," said Stardust. "Your voices are wonderful. It would be amazing if we could all sing together at the ancient Whispering Wall on Midsummer Day."

Misty looked thoughtful.

"I'll come if I can sing a duet with Honey," Goldie spoke up.

Honey shook her head sadly. "I'm sorry, but my voice isn't good enough for that."

"It would be if you practiced—and I can help you," replied Goldie.

"That's very brave of you," said Misty.

Honey pawed the ground. She took a

deep breath and quickly said, "Okay, I'll do it."

Misty touched her horn to Honey's, then she gracefully turned around to face the watching unicorns.

"These ponies have shown such courage by coming here today. And now Honey has shown even more bravery by agreeing to sing a duet with Goldie. Can you overcome your fears too?"

There were bright flashes of sunlight sparkling on golden horns as every unicorn dipped his or her head in agreement.

"Yes," they sang, their voices chiming like magical bells.

Misty nodded back at them proudly.

"Let's go to the castle," she said with a smile.

The late afternoon air seemed to shimmer with the beautiful voices as unicorns and ponies stood together and practiced their singing before the Whispering Wall. Sun streamed into the courtyard, its long, glittering fingers brushing the four golden horseshoes already hanging on the wall, making them sparkle and glitter with magic.

As the voices soared, Pippa stepped forward and hung the fifth horseshoe on Misty. Her fingers tingled with magic as the golden horseshoe met the golden horn. There was a brilliant flash of light, and Pippa shielded her eyes with her hands. Misty stood up on her back hooves and placed the horseshoe on an empty black nail.

Pippa's smile was so wide she thought her face might split in two.

"Five horseshoes safe," she whispered to Stardust.

"Five," Stardust echoed happily. "There are only three left to find now. We're going to do this, aren't we?"

Midsummer was in two days. Pippa felt doubtful. Could they really find all the horseshoes by then?

The unicorns and ponies finished their song and started a new one. Their voices swelled in the air, carrying Pippa's doubts away.

She nodded her head. "Yes!" she said confidently. "Yes, we are."

Chevalia Now!

EXCLUSIVE
INTERVIEW WITH
PRINCESS HONEY

by Tulip Inkhoof

Chevalia's Cloud Forest has long been thought to be haunted by ghosts. But today two brave ponies and one brave girl ventured into the mysterious forest and revealed its special secret: unicorns live there!

This reporter caught up with Princess Honey, who's been visiting her unicorn friend, Goldie, in the Cloud Forest ever since she was a young foal.

☆ **TI (Tulip Inkhoof):** Honey, how did you discover the secretive unicorns?

☆ **H (Honey):** First of all, can I just say that I *love* your purple hoof polish. It's so sparkly!

☆ **TI:** Oh, thank you—I visited the Mane Street Salon on my way to Stableside Castle.

☆ **H:** I love getting my hooves painted!

☆ **TI:** Me too! But let's talk about the unicorns. How did you find out about them?

☆ **H:** Right, down to business! Well, one day my class at Canter's Prep School went on a trip to the Savannah and I thought I could hear singing coming from the nearby Cloud Forest. As I trotted to the edge of the forest, I heard the loveliest songs floating out of it. I knew the legends about the forest, but these voices were so beautiful I didn't think they could possibly be ghosts, so I sneaked off and set hoof into the forest.

☆ **TI:** But weren't you frightened?

☆ **H:** Oh, I was, and I thought about turning around. Instead I sang back. I repeated the lovely song as I went into the mist—and I came face-to-face with a small unicorn!

3

☆ **TI:** How extraordinary!

☆ **H:** Mom and Dad used to tell us unicorn stories at bedtime, and I never thought they were real. But this unicorn was definitely real! She introduced herself as Goldie, and do you know what?

☆ **TI:** What?

☆ **H:** She looks a lot like me!

☆ **TI:** So you can confirm the rumor about the unicorn twins?

☆ **H:** Yes, all of the ponies on Chevalia have a unicorn that looks like them in the Cloud Forest. Even you, Tulip! It's a very special bond.

☆ **TI:** I wonder if my unicorn is an enterprising young reporter?

4

☆ **H:** Maybe! That first day in the forest, I met the unicorn twins for my entire  family, but as the unicorns were so shy, I promised them I wouldn't reveal their secret. Every once in a while, especially if I was feeling sad or if the salon couldn't fit me in for a hoof scrub, I'd trot up to the Cloud Forest for a unicorn adventure.

☆ **TI:** So what happened to make you bring Stardust and Pippa with you today?

☆ **H:** I was upset because Stardust was making fun of my singing so I ran away to the Cloud Forest, and Stardust and Pippa followed without me realizing. Pippa thought that if everyone was scared of the forest, then that might make it a good

hiding place for the golden horseshoes—
and it turned out she was right!

☆ **TI:** I hear that Pippa rescued a horseshoe
from a dragonfly nest, and then it was
nearly stolen by two
Night Mares who
go by the names
of Thunder and
Lightning?

☆ **H:** Yes, the Night Mares were crossing the
river to get away from us, but Misty saved
the day with her magical horn by making
the river freeze.

☆ **TI:** What a busy day! Well, I should let you
get back to singing practice.

☆ **H:** Yes, Goldie and I need to practice our
duet for the Midsummer concert! See you
there!

Princess Ponies

An Amazing Rescue

Chapter 1

Pippa and Stardust were racing along a track in the Wild Forest. The trees grew close together, their thick branches keeping out all but a few thin rays of sunlight. The only sounds were Stardust's snorts and the muffled thudding of her hooves on the leaf-strewn path. Pippa hung on to Stardust's mane, concentrating on the trees, ducking to avoid low-hanging branches.

Suddenly a slanting ray of sunlight lit the path ahead, revealing a fallen tree. Pippa gasped. The trunk was massive, wider than the castle's moat and taller than the Whispering Wall. But Stardust was going too fast to stop, and there was nowhere to turn.

"Hold tight," she snorted.

She lengthened her stride and Pippa's heart thumped in her chest. They were going to jump it! With trembling hands, Pippa gripped Stardust's snowy white mane even tighter. Seconds later the princess pony jumped. Air rushed at Pippa's face and, as they flew upward, her stomach dipped. Images of a gnarled wooden trunk and a jumble of leafy branches jutting out in all directions

flashed before her eyes. Surely the tree was too huge for Stardust to clear?

As Pippa's stomach lurched, she heard a low, rhythmic noise in the air. What was that? It sounded like an enormous pair of beating wings.

"Stardust!" Pippa's breath caught in her throat. "Are we flying?"

"Yes!" Stardust's voice was shrill with excitement.

Pippa glanced down—and immediately wished she hadn't. The tall trees below looked like little broccoli florets from up here.

"Isn't this wonderful?" Stardust asked.

Pippa's legs tightened around her friend's flanks. Stardust felt reassuringly warm and solid. But how could she be flying? Pippa looked around, but suddenly Stardust dived, pitching Pippa forward and over her head. She tumbled through the air, the breath rushing out of her as the ground sped closer in a kaleidoscope of greens and browns.

Thud! Pippa landed on something soft. Her head jerked back and her eyes snapped open. Blinking in the gloomy light, she was surprised to see that she was in her own bed in Stardust's tower room at Stableside Castle.

"Oh, I was dreaming."

Pippa lay still while her racing heart slowed. It was ages before it began to beat normally. Across the room Princess Stardust snuffled and snored as she slept. Pippa watched the first light of dawn nudge at the tower window. It was followed by a familiar, rhythmic beat. Sitting up, Pippa turned her head toward the window to listen.

"Wings!" she said, leaping out of bed and running to the window.

Standing on her tiptoes, Pippa peeped outside. The sky was still dark,

with a few stars twinkling in the distance. The beating sound grew louder and more urgent. It reminded Pippa that there was something she ought to be doing. Her head swam as she struggled to remember what. It came to her in a rush. It was the day before Midsummer and three of the golden horseshoes were still missing.

"We have to find them!" she whispered to herself.

Pippa's hands curled into fists. She had been brought to the enchanted island of Chevalia, inhabited by talking ponies, to do a very special job. The eight golden horseshoes that were supposed to hang on the ancient Whispering Wall in the castle's courtyard had gone missing.

Without them, the magical island couldn't survive. Pippa had vowed to find the horseshoes and return them to their rightful home in time for their magical energy to be renewed on Midsummer Day.

She stared out, searching for the source of the flapping sound. It was louder now and was making the windowsill vibrate. Pippa looked out the window and up to the right.

"Peggy!"

A huge, silver horse hovered in the sky. Pippa hadn't seen Peggy since she helped them retrieve the first missing horseshoe from the foothills of the Volcano.

"Hello, Pippa," Peggy said warmly. "Congratulations. Triton and Rosella, the seahorses, tell me that you've found five of the missing horseshoes."

Shame and failure washed over Pippa. She felt she didn't deserve to be congratulated.

"But there are still three missing," she exclaimed.

"It's not Midsummer Day yet," Peggy said calmly. "Maybe I can help you find another horseshoe. Come here, child, and I'll take you on a tour of the island."

Pippa quickly dressed in the riding pants and horseshoe-patterned top that had appeared overnight especially for her, laid out neatly on a chair.

Peggy hovered next to the window, her feathery wings outstretched like a

glider. Reluctantly, Pippa moved closer. Surely Peggy didn't expect her to climb out of the window and onto her back? Pippa recoiled at the thought.

"I can't," she squeaked. "Stardust is still asleep. What if she wakes and finds me gone?"

"Stardust will be asleep for ages yet.

If you're scared of falling then don't be. I won't let you fall."

Pippa's chest tightened. Scared didn't even come close to how she felt. She was terrified of heights, even though she'd been learning to overcome her fear.

"Come," Peggy said, her eyes gently encouraging Pippa.

Pippa hesitated—it was hard not to trust Peggy. Staring at the flying horse's silver chest, she edged closer to the window.

"Don't look down," Peggy whispered.

Pippa concentrated on Peggy's wide back, which was as comfy-looking as a sofa. Reaching out of the window, she took a handful of mane.

"I can do this," she said firmly.

Her hands trembled like feathers in the wind as she climbed out onto the tower's windowsill. Her thudding heart made it almost impossible to breathe. Pippa paused to fill her lungs with the chilly dawn air. Then, with her eyes still on Peggy's back, she prepared herself for her next move.

"One, two, three," she whispered.

Quickly, before she could change her mind, Pippa scrambled onto Peggy's back. Once on it, she was too afraid to move. Peggy turned her head to nudge Pippa's foot with her nose.

"Well done," she neighed. "Now hold on tight."

A warm feeling spread upward from

Peggy's touch, filling Pippa with confidence. She could do this!

The sun was slowly rising behind them, bleeding red and gold across the dark sky, as Peggy soared up and over the Fields. Pippa's confidence gradually grew, until she was brave enough to look down. The island, surrounded by shimmering sea, was bathed in the soft gold glow of dawn. Even the dark Volcano was wrapped in a golden light that hung like a huge scarf around its craggy shoulders. Pippa searched for the peak of the Volcano but the wooded slopes disappeared into a summit of swirling mist. It was so beautiful that it made her heart sing.

"How could anyone want this to

disappear?" Pippa knew that she would do anything to save Chevalia.

Peggy skimmed over the treetops as she carefully swooped over the island. Pippa strained her eyes for the slightest flash of gold that could signal the missing horseshoes. As Peggy completed her first loop of the island, she climbed higher then hovered over the Fields. Far below, the tiny ponies, opening up their shops on Mane Street, reminded Pippa of the plastic ones in her brother's toy farmyard.

"Pippa." Peggy's voice was low and urgent, and it cut into her thoughts. "I want to ask you something. Take your time before you answer me. Would you like to go home, to the human world?"

A wave of homesickness washed over Pippa. When she stopped to think about it, she missed her family and home a great deal, even though they weren't missing her since Chevalia existed in a time bubble. Pippa could stay for as long as she liked while no time passed in her own world.

"I can't leave now," she said.

"It would be safer if you did. We might not find the remaining horse-shoes and I can't guarantee your safety."

Pippa felt as if her heart was being ripped in two. Suddenly she craved the safety of her family, but then again, how could she leave Stardust and Chevalia when they needed her help more than ever? The seconds ticked by. Wordlessly

Peggy glided in huge circles over the Fields.

"I made a promise to find the missing horseshoes," said Pippa finally. "I'm not going home until I do."

Peggy flapped her wings in double time.

"Pippa MacDonald, you are a true pony lover and a very special friend of Chevalia," she snorted.

Chapter 2

Peggy flew over the island again, swooping even lower to help Pippa search for the missing horseshoes.

Keeping her eyes fixed on the passing landscape, Pippa asked her, "Why do you never land? Don't you get tired, staying in the air for so long?"

"I never used to get tired," said Peggy, "though recently my wings ache at night. But I can't land. The magic that lets me fly will vanish if I do and I'll become an ordinary pony."

"You'll never be ordinary," said Pippa.

Peggy's laughter sounded like music.

"A very long time ago, when Chevalia was just a small volcanic island, I was an ordinary pony. I was lucky enough to make a very special friend, a scientist-magician named Nightingale. This pony had amazing powers and a brilliant mind. She discovered the magical gold buried in the volcanic rock. Nightingale realized the potential of that special gold, and she had it mounted on the Volcano. Over time the island grew larger and more magical, until it finally blossomed into the Chevalia that we know and love today. Nightingale had created a paradise, but that wasn't enough for her. She wanted to share it with ponies from around the world."

Pippa listened intently to Peggy's tale.

"Nightingale knew that some ponies were badly treated and had unhappy lives. It was those ponies that she wanted to come and live on Chevalia. So she invented a magic flying potion. The potion was so strong that it allowed the pony who drank it to fly forever, provided his or her hooves never touched the ground. And there was more—by drinking the potion, the pony could give the temporary gift of flight to any pony whose nose she rubbed. Nightingale asked me to drink the potion so that I could fly to the human world and rescue any unloved or mistreated pony who wanted a better life. The potion also kept me young, so for hundreds of years I flew around the world rescuing ponies in need and bringing them here to Chevalia. Once they arrive and their hooves touch the land, their wings vanish. Then they're free to live here in happiness, as every pony deserves."

"That's an amazing story," said Pippa. "What a wonderful job to have."

"Yes," Peggy sighed. "I've enjoyed every moment of it. But my wings are not as young as they were. When they ache, I dream of a cozy stable with a deep straw bed where I can rest my tired bones." She laughed softly. "But I still love to fly and help ponies in need. And as long as there are ponies to be helped I shall stay airborne."

"And I thought you flew because you were too special to walk on the ground," said Pippa.

Peggy laughed again. "No pony is too special to walk and talk with others."

"It's a big responsibility," Pippa said, full of admiration.

"I made a promise to Nightingale and to Chevalia," said Peggy.

Pippa nodded. She understood. She'd made a promise to help Chevalia too.

After they'd flown in silence for a while, Pippa said, "I have to go back to the castle soon. Stardust will worry if she wakes up and sees that I'm not there."

At once Peggy banked left then headed directly to Stableside Castle.

"Don't worry, Pippa. I'll continue searching for the horseshoes from the sky."

"And I'll keep searching too—with Stardust, of course," said Pippa.

When they reached Stardust's tower bedroom, Peggy came to a sharp halt, sending Pippa flying through the air. It was just like her dream, only this time she sailed through the tower window before landing with a thump on her bed. She caught a flash of Peggy's shiny hooves as she soared into the air, her silver tail streaming behind her.

"What's all the noise about?" groaned the waking Stardust. Rubbing her eyes with her hooves, she struggled up.

"You'll never guess where I've been," said Pippa. "Flying around the island on Peggy's back looking for horseshoes!"

"Liar, liar, tail's on fire," Stardust said

with a giggle. "You're still in bed, silly. You must have been dreaming."

"It wasn't a dream," Pippa insisted, but Stardust said nothing as she combed out her mane.

Pippa climbed out of bed and went over to the dresser to help her.

"We're running out of time. We've

got to continue searching for the remaining horseshoes."

"I agree," said Stardust. "But breakfast first. I'm starving. You know I can't work on an empty tummy."

Pippa let out a long sigh. She desperately wanted to continue her search, but she knew that Stardust was right.

"Breakfast first then," she agreed. "Let's hurry."

Chapter 3

Pippa and Stardust made their way down the tower's spiral ramp to the dining room. Mrs. Steeplechase, the royal nanny, was striding up and down between the feeding troughs, snorting out orders to the prince and princess ponies.

"Let's go next to Cloud," Pippa said, concerned at how grumpy Stardust's sister looked.

The silver-gray pony was wearing a new tiara—gold, with pretty blue sapphires—instead of her usual wooden one that was decorated with acorns, but the sparking jewels couldn't hide her mood.

As Pippa and Stardust approached, Cloud tossed her head and walked away. Pippa's face fell.

"Don't mind her," Prince Comet said, closing the book he'd been reading while eating. Comet was a serious-looking pony with a dark brown coat and a thick, black mane and tail.

"Cloud can't help being grumpy. It's just the way she is," added Stardust.

Cloud stopped and turned back. "I'm not grumpy. I'm fed up. All everyone

talks about these days are the missing horseshoes and how Chevalia will fade away if they aren't found by tomorrow. Pah! Missing horseshoes, my hoof! It's just a silly story made up to frighten little ponies into behaving."

"It's not a story. It's a myth," said Comet.

"Same difference," argued Cloud. Irritably, she swished her long, gray tail as she hurried out of the dining room.

Comet shook his head. "It's not the same thing at all. Myths are so much more than make-believe—they originate from a popular belief. The ancient scrolls mention the power of the golden horseshoes. They're the key to Chevalia's survival."

Stardust took a mouthful of oats. She chewed them carefully before swallowing. "Cloud *is* always grumpy. Fact. That should be written in the ancient scrolls too."

Comet snorted with laughter.

"Has anyone tried to find out why she's grumpy?" asked Pippa.

Stardust stared at her. "There's no reason. It's just the way Cloud is," she replied.

"Well, maybe someone should ask her," Pippa said thoughtfully.

"Good luck with that. Don't be surprised if Cloud snaps your head off when you ask her." Stardust took another mouthful of oats.

Pippa reached for a bright red apple and polished it on her top.

"Is Cloud going to school now?" she asked.

"Not today," said Stardust. "That's one of the best things about the days leading up to Midsummer Day—we keep having holidays."

"But that doesn't mean you can

run wild for the day," snorted Mrs. Steeplechase.

Pippa jumped as the royal nanny appeared beside them. She listened patiently while Mrs. Steeplechase lectured them about behaving like proper princesses. When the nanny finally moved on, Pippa turned to Stardust.

"Wild!" she exclaimed. "I dreamed about the Wild Forest last night. We haven't searched there yet. Let's go there today."

Stardust's eyes sparkled with excitement. "Oooh! I love the Wild Forest. The ponies who live there have such fun. Maybe they'll let us play with them. After we've finished our search," she added quickly.

After breakfast Pippa and Stardust rushed out of the castle.

"Hop on my back," said Stardust. "It's so much fun when you ride me."

Pippa jumped onto Stardust and the pony took off at a smart trot, her long,

white tail flowing behind her. They cantered across the wide Fields and plunged into the Wild Forest. Remembering her dream, Pippa kept a sharp lookout for fallen trees. Occasionally she'd see a group of wild ponies playing together. Once Stardust headed toward them, but the ponies ran away amid snorts of laughter.

"I'm not supposed to play in here," said Stardust. "Mrs. Steeplechase says it's not princess-like to mix with the wild ponies. She also worries about the mud. It sucks you in then swallows you up. But we're here to look for the horseshoes so that's all right."

Stardust trotted deeper into the forest. It was on the side of a steep hill and they were traveling downward so Pippa had to lean back. The last time she'd been here with Stardust they'd been going the other way. Riding downhill at speed was much trickier. Pippa didn't want to fall off and risk landing in the dangerous mud.

After riding for a while, Pippa noticed a tree with a trunk that was twisted like a question mark.

"Haven't we passed that tree once already?" she asked.

Stardust glanced at it as she trotted past. "I don't think so," she replied.

"Well, we've definitely passed that tree there," Pippa said, pointing to a bleached-white tree trunk that stuck up in the air like a giant knitting needle.

Stardust stopped to examine the branchless tree. "Hmmm," she said. "That's been hit by lightning. And you're right. We did pass it earlier." She turned in a slow circle then stopped.

Pippa stared at the trees crowding in on them. The Wild Forest was dark and gloomy. Fear prickled up her neck.

Stardust seemed uneasy too. Her muscles twitched and suddenly she shivered. Pippa hung on tight as Stardust trembled.

Very quietly Stardust whinnied, "I think we're lost."

Chapter 4

Goosebumps formed on Pippa's arms, forcing the hairs to stand up in lines like soldiers. She breathed deeply, trying to squash the panic rising inside her.

"We're not totally lost," she said. Her voice came out in a squeak and she cleared her throat before continuing. "Uphill leads back to the Fields and downhill toward the beach."

"You're right," Stardust said, "but the forest is huge. We could walk for days without ever reaching the beach or the Fields."

A twig cracked behind her. Stardust turned around in time to see a silver-gray pony dashing through the forest. She was laughing so hard she didn't notice Pippa and Stardust.

"Catch me if you can!" she shouted, hopping over a fallen branch.

"Cloud?" Stardust said, her mouth open wide with shock.

"Coming to get you!" shrieked a familiar voice.

Stardust fell back, snorting with surprise, and Pippa blinked several times as a chestnut pony, wearing a satchel around her neck, chased after the silver-gray pony.

"That can't be Cinders." Pippa hesitated then added, "It is! It's Cinders and Cloud."

"They look like best friends," said Stardust.

She took off, chasing after them.

Pippa's wavy, dark hair streamed out behind her as Stardust ran through the forest. She could hardly believe it herself. Cinders never played with anyone. She was far too uppity for that, or so she'd thought. But here she was now, playing with Cloud in the Wild Forest.

"Look," Stardust snorted, suddenly changing direction.

Pippa's mouth fell open as a group of wild ponies ran past. They raced through the forest, leaping over fallen branches, jumping on top of tree stumps, and running up tree trunks to hurl themselves out of trees.

"That looks dangerous," gasped Pippa.

"It's called free-trotting," said

Stardust. "I've always wanted to try it but Mrs. Steeplechase won't let me. Look at that! Oh my goodness. They're never going to jump that ravine!"

The trees abruptly gave way to an enormous ravine with steep, craggy sides. Pippa felt nervous as Stardust trotted closer. It was a very long way down, and a river roared fiercely at the bottom. Stardust stopped closer to the edge than Pippa would have liked, but the free-trotting ponies were speeding up. Pippa covered her face with her hands, only managing to peer at the ponies through a gap in her fingers. There were loud snorts of laughter as, in groups of three, the wild ponies hurled themselves over the edge of the ravine. As the ponies jumped, their tails and manes streamed out like multi-colored flags in the wind.

Pippa couldn't breathe when she realized that Cloud and Cinders were jumping with them. Time seemed to stop as Cloud and Cinders launched themselves across the gaping chasm.

There were two loud thuds and thick clods of mud flew through the air. Pippa blinked, and when she looked again Cloud and Cinders were safely on the other side, blowing through their noses and laughing with the wild ponies.

"Awesome," she breathed.

Stardust danced on her hooves with excitement. "That was amazing. Did you see Cloud and Cinders jumping together? I'd love to try that," she added longingly.

"I bet they had lots of practice first," Pippa said anxiously.

Stardust giggled. "Don't worry. I'm not about to give it a go. That sort of jump must take ages to perfect. But how did Cloud and Cinders learn to do it?"

Stardust's eyes twinkled. "Unless that's what Cloud does when she goes off in a sulk. I bet she comes here to practice. No wonder she's so good—she's always going off in a huff!"

Stardust edged even closer to the ravine.

"Hi, Cloud," she called. "That was amazing."

Cloud turned around in surprise, and her face darkened with anger.

"Stardust!" she exclaimed. "Go away. This is *my* special place. Anyway, you're not allowed to play here."

Chapter 5

Cinders turned back to her friend, her eyes full of suspicion.

"Cloud," she groaned, "what did you invite them for?"

"I didn't," Cloud snorted, annoyed. "They must have followed me here."

"We didn't follow you!" said Stardust. "Well, only a little bit. We came to the Wild Forest to look for the missing horseshoes, but we found you instead."

Cloud stomped her hoof. "Great! And now you're going to tell on me."

"No," exclaimed Stardust. "I'm not a tattletale!"

"We saw your free-trotting and it was incredible," Pippa said, changing the subject. "It must have taken you ages to learn how to do it."

"Not really," replied Cloud. "The main thing is confidence. If you're not scared to try, then it's really easy. The wild ponies are brilliant teachers. They're patient and kind, not like grumpy old Mrs. Steeplechase."

"The wild ponies sound amazing," Pippa agreed.

Cloud's eyes twinkled. "They're very good friends of mine," she said.

"Not everyone likes them but that's because they don't know them. You've got to look past the outside—just because ponies are scruffy that doesn't make them bad. My wild pony friends are caring and generous. And they like me for who I am. They're not interested in titles—no one cares if I'm a princess here. This is the only place in Chevalia where I can be my real self. Free-trotting is part of that. It makes me feel alive. It makes me feel like I can fly, and I love that."

"I love flying too," said Pippa. She didn't add that she'd flown with Peggy only that morning in case it sounded like she was boasting.

Cloud shyly dipped her head. "Would

you like to come free-trotting with me?"

"I'd love to," Pippa said, tempted to accept Cloud's invitation. "But we need to find the three missing horseshoes, and time is running out."

"The missing horseshoes!" Cloud sighed. "I'm still not sure I believe in all that."

"Neither do I," Cinders chipped in. "Mom says it's all a load of garbage."

"But what if it is true?" Pippa asked quietly.

Cloud scuffed a hoof on the ground. "That old Whispering Wall doesn't look right without the horseshoes. I suppose we could help you search for them, just to make it look normal again—not because I believe in all that 'horseshoe magic.'"

"It could be fun," Cinders agreed. "I bet the wild ponies would help us too."

"Would they?" asked Pippa. "That would be great. The more eyes the better."

Only Stardust looked doubtful. "I don't know," she said. "We're not really supposed to be here. Maybe we should go back now."

"But you're here now," called out a cheeky young chestnut pony with a white blaze. "And I've seen you and that girl here once before."

Stardust blushed bright red. "You're right. Pippa and I took a shortcut through the forest the day she arrived on Chevalia."

"We don't mind," said the wild pony. "You're welcome to come here any-time you like. My name's Clipper. I can teach you to free-trot if you like."

Stardust's eyes widened. "Really? I'd love that."

"Stand back then," said Clipper. "I'll jump back over the ravine so we're on the same side."

Led by Clipper, the wild ponies, Cloud, and Cinders jumped the ravine.

Cloud trotted over to Pippa. "Would you like to ride on me while Stardust learns how to free-trot?"

"Yes, thank you," said Pippa.

She slid from Stardust's back and jumped onto Cloud's. The older princess pony was taller and broader than Stardust, and Pippa almost didn't make it. Clinging on to Cloud's gray mane, she pulled herself on in an undignified scramble.

"Well done," Cinders said, helping

Pippa up with a friendly nudge to her foot.

"Missing horseshoes, here we come," Cloud whinnied.

Cloud set off at such a high speed it made Pippa's teeth snap like a crocodile's.

"You're so fast," she squealed.

"This is the one place I can let my mane down," said Cloud. "If I didn't have the Wild Forest to escape to I'd go absolutely mad with boredom. I hate living in the Royal Court with all its stuffy rules and traditions. Here in the Wild Forest everyone is equal. I don't have to keep curtsying, and I don't have to wear that stupid tiara."

Pippa ran her hand down Cloud's

neck, feeling the princess pony's muscles rippling as she leaped from one obstacle to the next. There were plenty of low-hanging branches to land on and tree stumps to jump over, but Pippa liked it best when Cloud trotted up the trunks to hurl herself out of the trees. It made her stomach flutter with excitement.

"This is fantastic," she yelled in Cloud's ear, making her buck for joy.

A long time later, they trotted into a clearing. Everyone slowed to catch their breath and cool down.

"Well done—you're a fast learner," Clipper told Stardust.

"Watch out," Cloud said, suddenly swerving left. "Mud."

Stardust bumped into Cinders, knocking her satchel. "Sorry," she apologized.

"No problem," Cinders said, shrugging off her satchel. "You've just reminded me I was supposed to get rid of this old thing for Mom."

The wild ponies trotted on, but Stardust and Cloud waited for Cinders.

"Why does the Baroness want you to throw her satchel in the mud?" Pippa asked, curious. "It doesn't look that old."

"Mom's even stricter than Mrs. Steeplechase," said Cinders. "You do what she says without questioning her."

Pippa stared at the satchel. Something was bothering her, but she wasn't sure what. Images of her previous adventures with Stardust flashed through her mind—the Night Mares, the mysterious hooded pony, and all the nasty comments Divine had made each time they were successful in their search.

"What's inside?" she asked suddenly.

"I don't know," said Cinders. "Like I said, you don't question Mom."

"May I have a look?"

Cinders hesitated then passed the satchel to Pippa. "Why not? Mom didn't tell me I couldn't show anyone."

The satchel was surprisingly heavy. Pippa felt all eyes watching her as she opened it up. As the flap fell back a flash of golden light blinded her. She blinked as she carefully opened the satchel wider.

"One—no, *two* of the missing horseshoes," she exclaimed.

"No!" Cinders whinnied, the color draining from her face.

"Are you sure?" Stardust and Cloud crowded closer.

"I don't understand." Cinders had tears in her eyes. "Mom doesn't believe in the legend of the horseshoes, so why would she take them?"

"She almost had you bury them forever," Cloud said quietly.

There was a shrill neigh and a hooded pony crashed into the clearing. It thundered over to Pippa. She froze as the hooded pony tore the satchel out of her hands and threw it into the mud.

"Divine!" squeaked Stardust.

"Mom?" Cinders pushed the hood back from the pony's face.

"How could you?" shouted Pippa.

She lunged for the satchel. One moment it was floating in the mud but, just as she reached to save it, there was a loud sucking noise like water being pulled down a giant drain. The mud belched out one large, brown bubble then closed over the satchel, swallowing it whole.

The golden horseshoes were gone.

Chapter 6

Pippa stared in horror at the powerful mud.

"Oh no!" neighed Stardust.

Pippa couldn't let Chevalia disappear with the satchel. "The horseshoes!" she cried, leaping into the mud.

"Pippa, no!" shrieked Stardust.

Pippa wasn't thinking clearly as she plunged her hands into the thick mud, her fingers searching for the satchel.

"I've got it," she called. "I've got the strap."

But the mud had hold of Pippa. The more she struggled to pull her hands out, the farther the mud sucked her down.

Pippa froze, not wanting to risk being pulled down even more.

"How stupid of me!" she muttered. How could she have been so reckless?

But she wasn't the only one not thinking. Cloud launched herself into the mud to help Pippa. Somehow they managed to pull the satchel free and toss it to Stardust.

Divine jumped forward. "Silly little girl," she shouted. "This isn't your battle. Why can't you mind your own business and go back to where you came

from?" She snatched the satchel from under Stardust's nose and ran away into the forest.

Cloud and Pippa were sinking fast.

"Use my back as a stepping stone to get to solid land," Cloud shouted.

Using all her strength, Pippa reached out for a clump of Cloud's mane and pulled herself onto her back. The added weight made Cloud sink faster. Quickly Pippa jumped for dry ground, landing with a squish. Mud splattered from her feet, covering Stardust and Cinders. For once Cinders didn't seem to mind she was dirty. She raced to the nearest tree and began to gnaw at the lowest branch with her teeth.

"Help me," she grunted.

Pippa reached her first, closely followed by Stardust. They wiggled the branch up and down while Cinders continued to chew on it. At last it snapped free.

"Easy now," Cinders said, as she guided it back to the mud. She laid the branch over the mud like a bridge.

"Hold on to the end," she called to Cloud.

Cloud held on to the branch with her mouth.

"Ready, everyone? On the count of three, pull," said Cinders.

Pippa's fingers gripped the branch tightly. As everyone pulled, the bark cut into her hand. She winced but never let go even though it felt like her arm was going to be pulled off. The drag of the mud made Cloud feel ten times heavier than she really was. Sweat trickled down Pippa's face. Gritting her teeth, she pulled harder. There was a crack like thunder and the branch snapped. Pippa fell backward, and Stardust and Cinders almost fell over too. Cloud was sinking even farther into the mud.

Stardust bolted to the edge of the forest, where long vines trailed from the trees. Selecting the strongest-looking vine, she broke it off and brought it back to the mud.

"Catch," she said, throwing one end to Cloud.

The vine fell short. Stardust reeled it in and threw it again. By now Cloud's back had disappeared and the mud was creeping up her neck. Pippa fought back tears. She couldn't let anything happen to Cloud, especially as the pony had just saved her life.

"Let me," she said, taking the vine from Stardust.

Pippa took a deep breath as she aimed. The vine snaked across the mud and landed at Cloud's head. Gratefully Cloud caught it in her teeth.

"Pull," called Pippa. "Harder."

But it was no use. Cloud was stuck—and was sinking even deeper. She was going to disappear into the mud, and it was all Pippa's fault.

Suddenly, a familiar, rhythmic noise sounded in the air. Pippa glanced up.

"Peggy," she gasped.

The sun flashed on Peggy's silvery wings, filling Pippa with hope, as the flying horse dived for Cloud. She hovered above the ground and rubbed noses with the terrified pony. The mud began to shake and bubble. Pippa

stared in amazement as a set of wings broke through the surface of the mud.

"You've given Cloud wings to fly," she breathed.

"Yes," Peggy neighed. "I'm allowed to use my magic to help any pony in trouble, even if they already live here on Chevalia."

Cloud's eyes widened in surprise and at once she began flapping her wings, causing the mud to bubble like lava.

"Harder," Pippa encouraged her.

Cloud's new wings soon found a rhythm. Mud sprayed off her in all direc-tions, splattering everyone. Then, with an enormous *pop*, Cloud burst free.

"Hooray," cheered Pippa.

Cloud rose into the air but the mud

on her wings was making her fly crook-
edly. She rolled toward Peggy, slapping
her with a muddy wing. Caught off-
balance, Peggy fell backward and landed
on the ground. There was a loud *clap*
and a flash of brilliant green light.
Silence followed.

Everyone stared at Peggy. Her wings

had disappeared, leaving her as a pretty, silver-colored pony.

Cloud came over, squealing in horror. "What have I done? I'm so sorry. How can you ever forgive me?"

A slow smile spread across Peggy's face. "The power is yours now, Cloud. I bestow upon you the magical gift of flight. Use it wisely. There are many ponies in the human world who need help. Go and seek them out, and, by rubbing noses with them like I did to you, allow them to fly so that they may come here to the safety of Chevalia."

"If there still is a Chevalia," Stardust burst out. "Divine has run off with two of the horseshoes."

Cloud hovered above Peggy.

"Are you sure that's what you want?" Cloud asked. "I could rub noses with you and transfer the power back."

Peggy closed her eyes. "I've loved my job. But I've done it for hundreds of years, and lately I've grown tired. It's time to step down and let someone younger take my place—if you want to, that is?"

Cloud's silver-gray chest swelled with pride. "I do. I want it more than anything."

"Then the power is yours," said Peggy. "And will be for as long as you stay in the air."

Stardust was becoming impatient. "But what about the horseshoes?" she shouted.

"Can I make them fly?" Cloud asked, nodding at Stardust and Cinders.

Peggy smiled and whispered, "The power is yours."

Cloud flew to Stardust. Keeping her hooves above the ground, she rubbed noses with her sister. There was a crack and a flash of light. Stardust gasped.

"I've got wings!"

"Me too," Cinders cried, as Cloud rubbed noses with her friend.

"Hurry, Pippa! Climb on my back." Stardust hovered as low as she dared without touching the ground.

Pippa reached for a handful of mane and pulled herself up on Stardust's back.

"Ready?" asked Stardust.

"Let's fly," Pippa agreed.

Stardust flapped her enormous, feathery wings. The breeze fanned Pippa's face and lifted her hair as they rose into the air. Cloud and Cinders flew up next to them, weaving through the branches until they were flying above the trees.

"There's Mom," Cinders said, pointing

with one of her hooves to a tiny pony who was racing beneath them through the forest.

"After her," cried Pippa.

Side by side, the three ponies flew after Divine.

Chapter 7

The Baroness galloped through the forest. She kept glancing upward as she weaved through the trees. The satchel swung wildly from her mouth. It got snagged on a branch, but Divine yanked it free and galloped on.

"Hurry," urged Pippa. "She's getting away."

Stardust's wings beat faster, fanning cold air at Pippa and making her eyes tear.

Divine burst from the Wild Forest and onto the vast green Fields. Head down, she galloped straight across it. As she reached the other side, she darted toward a bush and disappeared down a hidden path.

"Where's she going?" Cloud wondered.

"That's a secret path to the Volcano," Cinders said as she flew after her mother, her wings creaking, her muscles straining with the effort.

"The Volcano? But why would she go there?" asked Stardust.

The flying ponies were finally gaining on Divine.

"Stop her," shouted Cloud.

As one, the trio of flying ponies

swooped in on Divine. Stardust and Cloud flew on either side of Divine while Cinders floated down in front of her mother.

With the ground approaching, Cloud called frantically, "Hooves up. Don't touch the ground."

Pippa was breathless with excitement and fear. Her knees gripped Stardust's flanks and her fingers were tightly wrapped around Stardust's mane.

Cinders hovered in front of Divine. "Stop!" she called. "Where are you taking the horseshoes?"

Divine tossed her head. "Get out of my way, foal."

"Please, Mom," begged Cinders. "Give the horseshoes back. No one needs to know it was you who took them."

"Never." Divine's eyes rolled wildly, showing their whites. "I'm taking the horseshoes home, where they belong."

"They belong on the Whispering Wall," said Pippa.

Divine laughed hysterically. Suddenly she rose up, and, shoving her face at Cloud, she rubbed noses with her. There was a loud crack and a blinding flash of light. Black dots swam in front of Pippa's eyes, and she rapidly blinked them away. A breeze fanned her face. Squinting at Divine, she saw that the pony was sprouting an enormous pair of chestnut-brown wings.

"No," Pippa breathed, an icy feeling shivering down her spine.

A wicked smile lit Divine's face. Experimentally at first, she flapped her wings. Her confidence grew as they lifted her into the air.

"The time has come," she whinnied, her shrill voice echoing weirdly as she flew higher above the narrow path, "to return this island to its original form!"

Pippa clenched Stardust's mane, fighting back tears, as Divine flew away triumphantly, the satchel swinging from her mouth.

"After her!" ordered Pippa.

"Yes, hurry," said Cloud.

In a whir of wings, the three ponies gave chase. Stardust's huge, white wings clapped together as she climbed higher. Pippa could hardly breathe. The ground whizzed away from her in a blurred mix of greens, browns, and sparkling blue sea. They flew over Stableside Castle, the eight flags fluttering from each of its toy-sized towers. Soaring after Divine was like playing a crazy game of tag. Each time Stardust, Cloud, and Cinders drew closer, Divine would suddenly change direction.

"Hold tight," Stardust shrieked, shooting left. Pippa slid right and barely held on.

Soon after that, Pippa began to cough. Smoke and ash hung in the air, tickling her nose and sticking to the back of her throat.

"We're almost at the top of the Volcano," Stardust said, coughing.

Pippa stared ahead as a tall cone of black rock rose from the tip of a cloud. Smoke belched from the Volcano. Sweat trickled down her face. She coughed again, clutching Stardust's mane as she used her other arm to cover her mouth.

Then, all at once, she had an idea.

"Cinders, Cloud," she whispered urgently. "Make Divine go higher."

Unquestioningly Cloud and Cinders did as she asked, but when Stardust tried to follow Pippa stopped her.

"Hide in the cloud above," she whispered.

Stardust's ears flickered quizzically as she followed Pippa's instruction.

When the misty cloud surrounded them, Pippa called out again, "There's Divine—below us. Can you fly down and surprise her?"

"I certainly can," Stardust said, dropping straight down.

Pippa kept her eyes on Divine's broad back as they flew down toward her. A dangerous plan was forming in her head. Pippa didn't share it with Stardust in case the pony tried to stop her.

"Three, two, one," she counted, then leaped from Stardust onto Divine.

"Pippa!" Stardust cried in horror.

Pippa smiled grimly as she landed on Divine's back.

"Get off, you horrible little girl!" Divine bucked wildly, twisting in the air to try and unseat Pippa.

With a viselike grip, Pippa hung on to Divine's mane with one hand as she swung down to grab the satchel with the other. Taken by surprise, Divine let it go. Pippa threw the strap over her head, then leaped onto Cloud's back—the

princess pony had been flying next to them. Pippa was trembling like crazy, but she'd made it!

"Noooo!" shrieked Divine. She reached for the satchel, but Pippa held it high above her head. Divine lunged again. Pippa swung the satchel around to the other side. Divine snapped her teeth, but Pippa ducked.

Cloud darted away, startling Divine, who continued flying, almost slamming straight into the side of the Volcano. With an angry screech, she folded her wings back, sticking out her hooves as she skidded to a halt. She was still traveling too fast. Her hooves pedaled the air and, with a crunch, she plowed into the side of the Volcano. There was a loud *pop*.

"Aaaaarghh!" Divine's furious screams rang out as her wings vanished.

Cinders flew behind Divine, holding her wings outward and upward to slow down. Pippa winced, but Cinders managed to stop, her hooves barely an inch from the ground. Sweat dripped from her heaving sides.

"That was close," she panted. "I thought I was going to crash into the Volcano."

"You silly little foal," spat Divine. "How could you betray me like this?"

"No, Mom," Cinders said, her voice trembling. "How could you betray Chevalia?"

"You don't understand," said Divine, her voice husky with regret. "Chevalia needs a change. But it isn't over yet."

The words hung in the air. Divine snorted then, turning around, she cantered up the Volcano's steep slope. Pippa watched until her large chestnut body was totally swallowed up by the misty cloud at the summit. Slowly she opened the satchel and removed the two golden horseshoes. As she held them up, the horseshoes glittered brightly, their magic spreading hope among the three ponies hovering in the air.

Stardust bucked triumphantly. "We've almost done it," she exclaimed.

"Almost," Pippa breathed. "But Divine is right. It's not over yet. There's still one horseshoe missing."

Chapter 8

Pippa held the horseshoes tightly as Stardust, Cloud, and Cinders flew back to the castle. They made a magnificent sight, flying like three huge birds over the island. Word soon spread and by the time they approached the castle, a crowd was waiting to greet them. The ponarazzi were there, pushing to the front of the crowd. Flying in a V-shape, the ponies soared over the clicking cameras, dipping their wings in salute as they flew onto the castle grounds. Pippa blinked furiously—the pop and flash of the ponarazzi cameras were as irritating as a cloud of gnats.

Stardust and Cinders landed in the Royal Courtyard to a gasp of admiration from the watching crowd. There was a loud crack as their hooves touched down. In a flash of light their wings vanished.

Stardust sighed happily. "That was such fun."

Cloud hovered several inches above the ground as everyone made their way to Queen Moonshine, King Firestar, and Peggy, who was wearing a new sash of deep green and a jade-studded tiara.

Stardust and Cinders curtsied so low their forelegs almost touched the rough stone floor.

"Welcome back," Queen Moonshine said, her voice as rich as warm honey.

Pippa sneaked a glance at the queen. She was looking even more beautiful than ever. Her long mane and tail flowed to the ground in a snow-white waterfall. Her golden coat shone from hours of grooming, and her hooves were painted with a pearly hoof gloss. In contrast, Peggy's gray coat was flecked with the white hairs of old age. Her muzzle was wrinkled and her hooves worn. She looked so much older than when Pippa had left her in the forest.

"You've been very brave," the queen said, looking first at Pippa, then Stardust, Cinders, and Cloud. "Peggy has told me everything—how you ventured into the Wild Forest then chased the Night Mares to retrieve two of the missing horseshoes."

Night Mares? Pippa opened her mouth to protest, but she felt Peggy's gaze boring into her. Peggy shook her head ever so slightly. Pippa snapped her mouth shut. Peggy looked away and Pippa was left wondering if perhaps she'd imagined the headshake. But Stardust, Cinders, and Cloud didn't correct Peggy either so Pippa decided she hadn't imagined it and remained silent.

"You may come down," Queen

Moonshine told Cloud. "The danger is over."

Cloud stayed in the air.

A *tsk* rang out behind her. The watching ponies parted as Mrs. Steeplechase pushed her way to the front.

"Your mother said to come down," the royal nanny said forcefully. "Hovering in the air isn't appropriate for a young princess."

Cloud smiled politely. "Peggy has lost her wings." She paused, her silence hanging in the air. "Chevalia needs a new flying pony—someone to go to the human world to save the neglected ponies. Someone to lead them to Chevalia, where they can be happy and free."

Mrs. Steeplechase inhaled sharply, but Queen Moonshine nodded, her eyes soft with understanding.

"Do you wish to take Peggy's place?" she asked.

"Yes." Cloud nodded fiercely. "More than anything."

"Then the role is yours with my blessing," said the queen. A tear formed in her eye and she blinked it away. "Just remember to come back and visit us often."

"I will." Cloud darted forward as if to nuzzle her mother with her nose, then quickly shied away.

Stardust and Cinders giggled, and even Pippa managed a smile at the thought of the queen suddenly sprouting wings. The smile faded quickly, though, as she stared at the two horseshoes weighing heavily in her hand. There was still one horseshoe to find. Without it there would be no refuge for any ponies on Chevalia.

As if hearing her thoughts, Stardust burst out, "There's only one day left to find the last horseshoe if Chevalia is to survive."

Murmurs of shock rippled through the watching ponies.

"No!" exclaimed Pippa. "It won't come to that. I won't let it. We *will* find the final horseshoe. I promise it'll be back on the Whispering Wall before sundown on Midsummer Day."

A cheer rose from the crowd. Pippa

felt sick with fear, but she forced herself to smile back.

"And now," said King Firestar, "let's hang the horseshoes in their rightful place on the Whispering Wall."

He nodded to Pippa but, instead of stepping forward herself, she waved Cloud closer.

"You should do this," Pippa said, handing her the horseshoes.

Cloud blushed, but her protests were drowned out by the cheering crowd.

"Cloud, Cloud, Cloud," they chanted.

Shyly, Cloud took the horseshoes from Pippa and flew to the wall. As the rays from the sun shone on the ancient stonework, Cloud hung the horseshoes back where they belonged. She flew

backward as they fizzled and flashed with magic.

The ponies cheered and stomped their hooves. Cloud tossed her head then soared upward. She circled the Royal Courtyard once then flew away.

Pippa realized she was holding her

breath. Letting it out, she turned to Stardust and hugged her tightly.

"We can do this," she vowed.

"We can," Stardust neighed. "For the love of Chevalia, we can."

Chevalia Now!

**EXCLUSIVE
INTERVIEW WITH
PEGGY**

by Tulip Inkhoof

After a lifetime in the air, Peggy has given up her wings and passed them—and the responsibility that comes with them—to none other than Princess Cloud, third in line to the throne of Chevalia. The mysterious former winged horse shared her secrets with me as she curled up on a straw sofa and sipped apple-spice tea.

☆ **TI (Tulip Inkhoof):** Peggy, can you please tell our readers how you came to be a winged horse?

☆ **P (Peggy):** It was a long, long time ago, my dear—back then, Chevalia wasn't much more than a volcanic rock in the sea. My friend Nightingale was a brilliant scientist-magician. She found a way to increase the island's size and magic, and she was determined to make it a safe haven for ponies from the human world who were treated poorly. Nightingale developed a magic flying potion that gave me wings, and for hundreds and hundreds of years I flew all over the human world, rescuing neglected ponies and bringing them here.

☆ **TI:** Why haven't we been able to meet you until now?

☆ **P:** Well, Tulip, an unfortunate side effect of Nightingale's potion was that I couldn't set my hooves on land. If I had, I'd have lost my wings. That was something I had to sacrifice in order to help other ponies.

☆ **TI:** Did that make you sad?

3

☆ **P:** Yes and no. I've always taken pleasure in seeing the rescued ponies have long, fun-filled lives on Chevalia. In fact, I brought your great-great-grandmare to this island—I can still remember it like it was yesterday. She was curious like you, but treated poorly in the human world. I found her tied to a post in a busy, crowded town. When I rubbed noses with her, she grew wings like mine, although hers were temporary, and together we flew to Chevalia, where she touched down and started a new life. It fills my heart with joy to know that I've helped achieve Nightingale's dream for Chevalia. But, I must admit, occasionally I felt a small pang of envy when I watched ponies

4

galloping and frolicking. Sometimes I wished I could just land and have a good canter myself.

☆ **TI:** And now you can!

☆ **P:** Yes, that's right. Another pony—a very brave pony—has taken on the wings of responsibility.

☆ **TI:** So it's true? You can confirm that Princess Cloud has become the new Peggy?

☆ **P:** Cloud is the new Cloud! She is her own pony, and I'm sure she'll fulfill her duties admirably.

☆ **TI:** But she's always been the grumpiest of the Royal Ponies!

5

☆ **P:** I believe there's good in all ponies, and I suspect that Cloud has been misunderstood by some of us. She craves a life of adventure and travel. Being cooped up in Stableside Castle, with its many rules, was too strict for such a life-loving pony.

☆ **TI:** I've never thought about it like that.

☆ **P:** You never truly know a pony until you step into their horseshoes, young Tulip Inkhoof.

☆ **TI:** And please tell us how you met Pippa MacDonald. I understand that you helped her retrieve the first magical horseshoe?

6

☆ **P:** Yes, I noticed that Pippa and Stardust were searching for something in the foothills of the Volcano, and I spotted something sparkly on a ledge. Luckily Pippa realized that I was trying to point it out to them.

☆ **TI:** You've gotten to know Pippa over the past few days, haven't you? Can you offer us any insights about her?

☆ **P:** Pippa is very loyal to her friends and those in need. I've been very impressed with her, especially this morning when I told her that she was free to return home if she wanted and that it would be safer for her there. She chose to stay and honor her promise to help Chevalia. The island needs bravery like hers now more than ever.

☆ **TI:** Well, Peggy, thank you so much for taking the time to talk to us. I hope you're enjoying being back on solid ground!

Princess Ponies

Best Friends Forever!

Chapter 1

A high-pitched cry woke Pippa. Throwing the covers back, she was out of bed even before she'd properly opened her eyes. In the enormous bed opposite hers, Princess Stardust was tossing about, thrashing her hooves and sobbing like a little foal.

Pippa went to comfort her best friend.

"Stardust, what's wrong?"

"No," Stardust cried, her breath coming in noisy snorts.

Gently, Pippa shook her friend awake.

"It's all right," she soothed. "You're safe now. It was just a bad dream."

Stardust struggled up, sleepily squinting at Pippa through the darkness as if she couldn't quite remember who she was. Pippa smoothed a tangle of white hair away from the princess pony's eyes.

"Better now?" she asked.

Stardust nuzzled at Pippa's hand.

"I was dreaming," she said flatly. "It was awful. It was Midsummer Day and we hadn't found all the missing horseshoes. The moment the sun set everything went completely black and there was a terrible roaring sound. Stableside Castle collapsed and the island shriveled up, leaving nothing but a lump of volcanic rock. All the ponies were huddled together on a tiny piece of land surrounded by the sea. The tide was coming in, swirling around our hooves and rising quickly up our legs. There was nowhere to go to escape the water. Baroness Divine had wings and she flew over us, shrieking with laughter and telling us that from now on we must wear hoods and not tiaras."

Stardust stumbled out of bed, picked up a comb, and halfheartedly tugged it through her mane.

"We're not going to let that happen!" Pippa said, taking the comb and brushing Stardust's mane with long, calming strokes.

"You're such a good friend," Stardust neighed. "And perhaps we *can* find the last horseshoe."

Pippa hugged Stardust and walked over to the tower window.

"It's dawn," she said, pointing at the streaks of pink that stained the dark sky.

Stardust picked up her pink jeweled tiara from the dresser and hurriedly placed it on her head between her ears. Grabbing a towel, she gave her hooves a quick polish. Usually Stardust spent ages getting ready, so Pippa could tell that the nightmare had really frightened her.

Pippa reached for the clothes that

had magically appeared overnight and were laid out in a neat pile on the dresser—her new outfit was a pretty striped top and leggings.

"I'm ready," Pippa said, shoving her feet into sandals.

Stardust hesitated at the bedroom door.

"Pippa," she whispered, her brown eyes suddenly looking too large for her face. "What if we don't find it in time?"

"We will," Pippa said, her confident tone masking her own fear, "if we work together!"

Six days ago Pippa had just arrived at the seaside for a vacation with her family when two giant seahorses magically whisked her away to Chevalia, an island inhabited by talking ponies. There she had learned that the enchanted island was in grave danger. Eight golden horseshoes were supposed to hang on an ancient wall in the castle's courtyard. Every Midsummer Day the horseshoes' magical energy was renewed by the sun, ensuring that the island continued to thrive. But the horseshoes had been stolen and Pippa learned that it was her quest to find them and bring them home in time for Midsummer Day. If she failed, Chevalia would fade away.

With Stardust's help she had managed to find seven of the missing horseshoes, but now Midsummer Day was here and if Pippa didn't find the last one before sunset then it would all have been for nothing. Fear gripped her stomach like an icy hand. Leading the way out of the bedroom, she started to run down the tower's spiral ramp.

"Breakfast first," Stardust said, nosing open the dining room door.

Pippa was desperate to get going, but Stardust was right—they needed a good breakfast before beginning their final search.

Pippa was surprised to find that they weren't the only early birds— Stardust's brothers and sisters were already at their feeding troughs. No one seemed to be eating much, though. Princess Crystal rolled an apple around three times without even taking a bite, and Prince Comet's hot oatmeal grew cold while he listlessly flicked through a book.

"It's the last day today," Princess Honey said bravely, as Pippa and Stardust squeezed in beside her.

"Please don't start to worry yet," Pippa said.

She was shocked by Honey's untidy

appearance. Pretty Honey usually took such care of herself and was a regular customer at the Mane Street Salon, but this morning her mane was tangled and she wasn't wearing any hoof polish.

Pippa ate a dish of fresh fruit salad without tasting any of it.

"We should go up the Volcano today," she declared. "I bet that's where Divine has hidden the last horseshoe."

Yesterday Stardust and Pippa discovered that it was Baroness Divine, one of the queen's advisers, who had stolen the horseshoes. She foolishly believed that she could make a better life for herself without the Royal Ponies.

"That's if she hasn't already destroyed the horseshoe," Stardust said sadly.

Comet snapped his book shut. "I don't understand it. I thought every adult pony had read the ancient scrolls, but clearly Divine hasn't," he said. "If she had read them then she'd know how, a long time ago, Chevalia was little more than a volcano surrounded by the sea. It's the eight golden horseshoes that allowed it to grow into the wonderful island it is today, and they must have their magical energy renewed for all our sakes."

"Peggy told me that story yesterday," said Pippa. "She also mentioned her friend Nightingale, the scientist-magician."

Comet nodded. "Yes, it was Nightingale who discovered the magical gold buried in the volcanic rock. She used it to fashion the horseshoes."

"Mom used to tell me that story at bedtime, but I thought it was just a story for little foals." Stardust stared around the dining room. "Where is Mom? Is she still in bed?"

"Mom and Dad were up long before us," Crystal answered. "I think they went to the courtyard."

"Let's go and find them," Stardust said, leaving most of her breakfast untouched.

Queen Moonshine and King Firestar were indeed in the courtyard, standing close together and staring sadly at the ancient Whispering Wall. Seven horseshoes sparkled in the early morning sun, but in spite of their brightness, Pippa's eyes were drawn to the gap where the eighth horseshoe should have been hanging. The bare space made her feel like a failure.

A shadow fell over the courtyard. Glancing up, Pippa saw Princess Cloud hovering above her in the air.

Queen Moonshine called out a greeting to her daughter, and Cloud swooped lower, making sure she kept her hooves away from the stone floor,

because touching down would mean losing her wings.

"I've got a plan," the queen said urgently. "Cloud, if you rub noses with every pony on the island then, come sunset, when the island begins to fade, everyone could fly away to safety."

"But that would take Cloud ages," squeaked Stardust.

"And where would the ponies go?" asked Pippa.

"They could find homes in the human world," the queen said.

Pippa shook her head. "Many of the ponies came here from the human world because they were neglected or treated badly there. We can't send them back again. And it isn't over yet—there's still time to find the last missing horseshoe."

"Pippa MacDonald, you've already faced so many dangers in your quest, and Chevalia is already in your debt. It's not right for us to ask even more of you."

"I'm not giving up now." Pippa's eyes burned with determination. "I promised to save Chevalia and I will!"

"Stardust," said the queen, "make your friend see that it's too dangerous."

Stardust tossed her head. "No, Mom. Pippa is right. We can't give up now, not when we're so close to saving Chevalia."

The queen sighed in acceptance.

Reaching out, she nuzzled Stardust and Pippa closer and hugged them tight.

"Stardust, you're the bravest foal I know. And you, Pippa, are the most courageous girl."

Pippa blushed.

"You haven't met any other girls," she said modestly.

"I don't have to," the queen said with a smile. "So where will your search take you today?"

"The Volcano," Pippa said immediately. "That's where the hooded pony ran to with the horseshoes we found yesterday, which suggests the eighth one is hidden there as well."

Pippa knew that if she said it was Divine who had stolen the horseshoes, the queen wouldn't believe her. Pippa would have to prove it.

"Then you know your path," said the queen. "Good luck, Pippa. Good luck, Stardust. Be safe."

Chapter 2

Pippa rode Stardust out of the castle and over the drawbridge, toward the base of the Volcano. As they began climbing the rugged foothills, the Volcano towered above them, its fiery top illuminating the sky. Now and then a puff of smoke rose in the air, spilling red cinders that drifted over the Cloud Forest and onto the lower slopes.

"It's getting hotter the closer we get

to the Volcano," Stardust said, stopping to catch her breath.

"I'll walk," Pippa said, starting to slide from Stardust's back.

"No," the princess pony said quickly. "I like it when you ride on me. It feels right."

She shied, narrowly avoiding a cloud of sparks as they shot to the ground.

"Even the Volcano feels angry. Maybe this really is the end for Chevalia."

"Never," Pippa said forcefully.

They continued in silence and soon they entered the mysterious Cloud Forest, home to the secretive unicorns. The forest felt cool and fresh. Pippa loved the way the sunlight filtered through the ancient trees, dotting the path with golden puddles of light. Stardust slowed down, weaving a careful path through the forest to avoid the enormous vines that trailed from branches like long snakes. They were over halfway through the forest when the hairs on Pippa's neck rose and her arms tingled with goosebumps. Convinced she was being watched, she looked around.

"What's wrong?" asked Stardust.

The forest around them was silent and still. As they stared into the cloudy gloom suddenly something jumped from a tree and stood on the path ahead. Stardust flinched then burst out laughing.

"Misty!" she cried.

Pippa appreciated once more just

how similar Misty was to Stardust. The unicorn was almost identical to her friend, from the tilt of her head to the tip of her snow-white tail. The only differences were the pretty golden horn on the top of Misty's head and their size—Misty was the size of a large dog.

"Hello!" Misty's musical voice bubbled with excitement. "Is it time already? Have you come to get us for the Midsummer Concert?"

Stardust shook her head sadly.

"I'm sorry, Misty, but there might not be a concert now. One of the horseshoes is still missing."

"No!" Misty gasped. "But it's Midsummer Day."

"That's why we're here. We're on our way to the Volcano—we think the horseshoe could be hidden there," Pippa said.

They quickly told Misty everything that had happened since the unicorns had helped them retrieve a missing horseshoe from the Cloud Forest.

"That's awful." Misty's eyes were wide with alarm. "I'm coming with you."

"It might be dangerous," Stardust warned her.

"It'll be more dangerous if the horse-shoe isn't found," Misty answered.

The trio set off at a brisk trot. It was fun having Misty with them. She knew the Cloud Forest like the back of her hoof and showed them a much quicker route through it. But it was still a long way.

Finally, they emerged from the treeline at the base of the Volcano and continued up its blackened slopes. The ground grew hotter, and Stardust and Misty hopped from hoof to hoof, trying to avoid stepping on the lumps of hot volcanic rock. The path twisted and turned and, as they trotted around a corner, Stardust came to an abrupt halt. Misty almost ran into her and only just stopped in time. A giant river of lava blocked the path. Pippa turned her face away from the fiery heat rising from the bubbling red liquid.

"That was close," Stardust said, carefully stepping backward. "We'll have to find another way around."

Pippa considered the bubbling lava, which stretched as far as she could see in both directions.

"That could take ages," she said. "It would be much quicker to cross it."

Her brain whirred with images as she tried to work out a solution. Luckily one came to her.

"Misty, could you freeze the lava with your magical horn?"

"I've never frozen something so hot before," Misty said doubtfully. "But I'll try."

Bravely, she stepped right up to the edge of the flowing lava.

"Careful," Pippa warned as a shower of sparks cascaded to the ground.

Misty lowered her head until the tip of her horn touched the lava. She winced then backed away.

"It's not working," she said sadly. "It's too hot and it burned me. Plus, I can sense that the lava has a magic of its

own. My magic would never be strong enough to freeze it."

As if the lava river was aware of its audience, it began to hiss. Bubbles rose to the surface, rapidly growing to the size of balloons before popping. They smelled of rotten eggs.

Stardust wrinkled her nose.

"Phooey! That's disgusting."

"We're going to have to jump it," Pippa said at last.

"I can't! It's too wide," Stardust squeaked.

"But there isn't another way around."

Stardust edged away from the hissing lava.

"'I'm sorry, Pippa, but I can't. It's much too wide."

"I bet you could if you tried. You jumped much farther than this yesterday when the wild ponies taught you how to free-trot."

Stardust stared at the lava rolling across their path. "Did I?" she said in a small voice.

"Yes, you did," Pippa said encouragingly, stroking her mane.

"But I'm scared!"

"I know," said Pippa. "But I've been scared so many times during our adventures, and I always knew you'd help me. Why don't we practice first? My mom always says *practice makes perfect*. Look— there are lots of boulders to jump over in preparation."

"All right," Stardust said finally.

Turning away from the lava, she began to hop over boulders, starting with the smaller ones. Each time she cleared one, Pippa cheered loudly. Misty joined in, stomping her hooves excitedly. Stardust's confidence grew, until soon she was jumping large boulders, clearing them with ease.

"Faster!" urged Misty. "The faster you run at the jump, the easier it is. Watch me."

Misty galloped toward a boulder almost twice her height. She cleared it with a triumphant flick of her hind hooves. Stardust stared in amazement. Singling out a boulder almost three times her height, she pawed at the ground then took off at a gallop.

"Brilliant!" Pippa shouted, as Stardust cleared the boulder with half a yard to spare.

Stardust pulled up, her sides heaving as she struggled to catch her breath.

"I'm ready," she said when she was breathing normally again.

A shiver of fear ran down Pippa's spine. Now that the moment had come to jump the lava river, *she* didn't want to do it.

Swallowing back her panic, she said, "Let's do it for Chevalia!"

Stardust turned away from the lava river. She went so far away from it that for a second Pippa wondered if she was running away. Then she turned on her hind hooves. Taking a deep breath, she put her head down and galloped toward the lava. A stride's length away she jumped, muscles bunching as she launched herself skyward. Pippa's face and arms glowed in the fiery heat beneath her. She held her breath, hardly daring to look down. Stardust hit the ground with a thump and galloped

several strides before she was able to pull up.

"We did it," she gasped.

"*You* did it," Pippa corrected her.

"We!" Stardust shouted to make her voice heard over Misty's triumphant cheers. "That was teamwork. I could never have done it without your help."

"We help each other all the time," said Pippa.

"I know," Stardust said happily. "It's what best friends do."

"It's my turn now," called Misty.

Stardust turned to watch the little unicorn run at the lava. Her golden horn bobbed up and down as she ran toward the molten river. There was a determined sparkle in her eye as she took off. She cleared the lava in one giant leap and her smile was brighter than the morning sun as she landed gracefully.

Pippa and Stardust cheered, but there was no time to rest. The three friends continued steadily up the Volcano.

"How much farther?" Stardust asked.

"We're nearly there," said Misty.

As the climb became steeper, Stardust and Misty fell silent, saving their energy for the ascent. Sweat trickled from Pippa's scalp and ran down her forehead into her eyes. Her wavy hair felt limp, like seaweed stranded on the beach. She pushed the hair from her face. What would they find at the top of the Volcano? With the hungry, red flames belching skyward, it was hard to imagine anything existing up there at all. The path continued to wind until, rounding another bend, Stardust stopped sharply.

"What's that?"

"It's a castle!" Pippa said, her heart pounding against her ribs.

Ahead of them was the biggest castle she'd ever seen, built into the face of the Volcano. Its towers loomed above them, with their tall, slit windows staring out like many eyes. Ebony towers spiked upward from behind a solid jet wall. A massive drawbridge was drawn up, preventing intruders from crossing a moat of bubbling orange-red lava and reaching an enormous, coal-colored door.

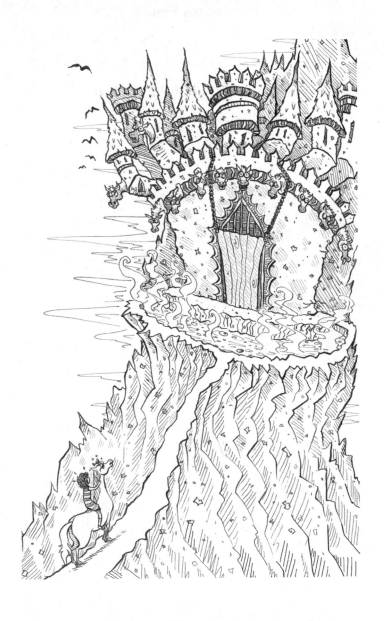

The whole place had a forbidding look. Even the craggy stone walls seemed to shout, "*Go away!*"

Stardust gave a huge, sad sigh.

"I don't believe it. We've come all this way and now we can't get in."

Chapter 3

Pippa squinted, scanning the Volcano Castle for a way in. She spotted guard ponies staring down over the walls.

"Look," she said, pointing. "The guards have seen us. They're lowering the drawbridge."

Two stern-faced Night Mares, wearing black sashes encrusted with diamonds, were letting the drawbridge down.

"Why would they do that right away,"

Pippa asked, "unless they're expecting us?"

"You mean it could be a trap?" Stardust asked, her voice squeaky with fear.

"Maybe—perhaps Divine guessed that we'd come after her."

"We don't have to go in," Misty said, taking dainty steps backward.

"We do," said Pippa. "It's our best chance of finding the last horseshoe."

As the drawbridge lowered over the moat, the guard ponies motioned for them to cross it and come up. Stardust stepped forward, and, after a hoof beat's hesitation, Misty followed. The flapping of wings made Pippa look up.

Something soared overhead and was gone in a flash. She gazed at the sky but there was nothing there. She gripped onto Stardust's mane as the princess pony trotted across the rattling drawbridge.

"Welcome, strangers," neighed the guards.

"Hello," Stardust whinnied back. "Please, can we come in?"

The Night Mares exchanged a grin.

"Of course," said the taller one. "It's a pleasure to have you here. It's not often that we get to welcome visitors."

Pippa could feel Stardust shaking beneath her. Taking a deep breath to steady her own trembling hand, she patted Stardust's neck. Bravely Stardust stepped up into the castle, which appeared to be the home of the Night Mares. Having passed through the enormous door, they found themselves in a courtyard.

"It's just like the one back home, only there's no Whispering Wall," exclaimed Stardust.

"There's no wall at all," said Pippa.

The courtyard stretched away and opened out into a long, stone balcony that overhung a huge pool of bubbling lava. Tearing her eyes away from the smoldering pool, Pippa stared upward and saw the blue sky dotted with fluffy, white clouds.

"This must be the heart of the Volcano," she whispered.

Her eyes widened as she took in their surroundings. The lava pool was indeed the very center of the Volcano, with a whole world carved into the rock around it. Pippa saw caves of all sizes linked by walkways of black stone. There were spires decorated with scary stone pony gargoyles that spat rivers of molten lava into the pit below. There were graceful arches and stone pillars all elaborately carved with the heads of ponies. The lava pool lit the caves, towers, and arches with a soft red glow. Pippa shivered despite the heat.

"Look how busy everyone is," Misty said in wonder.

Ponies bustled about, nodding to each other as they hurried past. Pippa gripped Stardust's mane as two familiar ponies trotted by.

"Look!" she gasped. "That's Nightshade and Eclipse."

"Hey, you!" Stardust shouted. "You stole our first horseshoe."

Several ponies stopped and stared, but Stardust ignored them and kept shouting until Nightshade turned around. She trotted over, closely followed by Eclipse.

"We did not," she said angrily. "The Mistress gave us that horseshoe. She said it belonged to her and that we must hide it for a game."

"That's not true," Stardust said, shaking her head. "The Mistress stole all eight horseshoes from the Royal Family. She took them from our ancient Whispering Wall, where they've hung for centuries."

"Are you sure?" asked Eclipse. "But the Mistress is our loyal protector— she wouldn't steal anything."

"The horseshoes belong here, where they were made," Nightshade argued.

"They were made here," agreed Stardust, "but they truly belong on the Whispering Wall. It's written in the

ancient scrolls. If you don't believe me then check."

"Ancient scrolls? I've never heard of any scrolls," Nightshade said. "And you shouldn't go around shouting at ponies that they're thieves," she added angrily. "Is that how they teach Royal Ponies to behave at Stableside?"

Pippa could see that the argument was going nowhere and that Nightshade was getting angry.

"Stardust didn't mean to call you a thief," Pippa said apologetically. "We're just really worried about the horseshoes—the last one must be found before the end of the day. We didn't know anyone actually lived inside the Volcano. It's amazing here—I'd love to look around."

Pippa smiled shyly and Nightshade smiled right back.

"Thank you. I think it's beautiful, but our home isn't to everyone's taste. I could show you around if you like?"

Pippa's face lit up.

"Yes, please!"

Eclipse stepped forward, staring at Pippa through her long, shaggy mane.

"You're from Stableside, aren't you? Those ponies are so stuck-up. They think they're the only ones with a proper castle. You wait till you see what we have here. Our castle is the best! It doesn't get much grander or older. This castle was here long before Stableside. It's the very heart of Chevalia."

"Really?" Pippa frowned. "So why would you want to destroy the island?"

Eclipse looked at Nightshade, who shrugged.

"What are you talking about?"

"The horseshoe that you were hiding for a game," Pippa said carefully, "is definitely one of the eight magical horseshoes that should hang on the ancient Whispering Wall. The scientist-magician Nightingale wrote in her scrolls that Chevalia can only survive if the horseshoes' magic— and the love they capture from pony and horse lovers around the world— is renewed by the rays of the sun every Midsummer."

Eclipse's eyes widened in alarm.

"What?" she whispered. "Is that really true?"

Pippa nodded.

"Then the Mistress has misled us." Nightshade looked ready to burst into tears. "She told us that the horseshoes were symbols of power and that by hiding them, Chevalia would return to its former glory, where the Volcano was the heart of the island and every pony was equal."

"Every pony should be equal," Pippa agreed, "but stealing the horseshoes isn't going to help. If you read the ancient scrolls, you'll realize that before Nightingale created the horseshoes, the island was just a small lump of volcanic rock—there was no former glory!"

"We must find the eighth missing horseshoe," Stardust said urgently. "We think it's here somewhere but we don't know where to look."

"We'll help," Nightshade said immediately.

Eclipse jumped up and when she spoke her voice was high with excitement.

"I think I know where it is. Nightingale had a laboratory hidden deep in the Volcano. The Mistress spends all her time there—she locked herself inside it all last night. I bet that's where she's hidden the last horseshoe. Follow me and I'll show you."

Eclipse took off at a smart trot. In single file, Nightshade, Stardust, and Misty hurried after her along several winding stone walkways and tunnels. The tunnels led to one side of the Volcano's inner rim and a series of caves.

"Nightingale's laboratory is in the last cave," Eclipse said, panting slightly as she walked around the puddles of lava and the black boulders littering the ground.

Eventually they came to an archway with a stone door and an iron latch. Eclipse flipped the latch up and pushed.

The door opened with a groan. In silence everyone walked inside, and Pippa dismounted from Stardust. Long benches covered with glass beakers that were coated with dust lined the middle of the cave. There were test tubes everywhere, filled with brightly colored liquids. Pippa's throat tightened at the acid smell of chemicals. A huge cream scroll tied with a dark pink ribbon lay on top of a wooden desk. Pippa's eyes were drawn to it. Was that the original ancient scroll or just a copy? Next to it, in a frame made from volcanic rock, was a picture of a stocky pony with bulging eyes.

"Divine?" Stardust asked, stepping forward.

"No, it's Nightingale," Nightshade corrected her. "The Mistress is a direct descendant of Nightingale. But, yes, they're very similar."

There were more portraits of Night-ingale on the walls, hanging in ornate

gold frames. The last picture had a modern frame and was of a smaller pony with eyes that protruded even more.

"That's Divine," Pippa exclaimed, pointing. Her voice rose suddenly. "And hanging above the picture is the last horseshoe!"

"Yes it is."

The voice that came from the doorway sent shivers racing along Pippa's spine. It was Baroness Divine.

"I've been expecting you." Divine smiled evilly. Throwing back her head, she laughed triumphantly, then she shouted, "Guards, seize them!"

Chapter 4

A group of Night Mares, wearing the guards' uniform of diamond-encrusted black sashes, charged into the laboratory and surrounded Pippa, Stardust, and Misty. They marched them outside and into a long, dark tunnel lit by flickering torches. As the tunnel twisted and turned it kept splitting into more passages.

"Left, right, right, left, left, left,"

Pippa murmured to herself as she tried to memorize the route they were taking.

They were traveling downhill and, after entering a very narrow tunnel, they finally arrived at their destination.

"The dungeons," Stardust neighed, her breath catching.

The guards roughly nudged the trio into the same cell. The door clanged shut and the key scraped in the lock.

Divine's hoof steps rang out mockingly as she started to trot away.

"You've failed." Divine laughed.

"Wait!" cried Pippa. "Why are you doing this to us?"

Divine turned around to face them. Stopping, she said, "Nightingale may be my distant ancestor, but she was a fool. When she found magical gold in the Volcano she fashioned it into two sets of symbolic horseshoes, one set each for the king and queen of the new island of Chevalia that the horseshoes went on to create. The island was a place where all ponies could be equal. But how could that ever be when Nightingale had decreed that there would be a king and queen? Far better, I say, that the island remains a volcanic rock, led by only one pony. My plan is to destroy the last golden horseshoe so that Chevalia will return to what it was—a simple place with no Royal Court or princess ponies. There will be just one leader. Me. I shall rule the new volcanic island."

Stardust let out a loud sob then bravely swallowed to stop any more from escaping.

"How are you going to destroy the horseshoe?" asked Pippa. Her heart hammered in her chest as she tried to buy some time.

Divine's eyes glowed in the torchlight.

"I plan to throw it into the heart of the Volcano, where the hot lava will melt it."

"Won't that be dangerous?" Pippa asked. "What about the magic locked inside the horseshoe?"

"Enough!" roared Divine. "My plan is nearly complete. I don't have time to waste talking to a silly little girl."

The Baroness walked away, the

guards following, their hooves echoing on the rough floor.

Stardust huddled in the corner of the cell and began to cry. Pippa wrapped her arms around her friend's neck. She buried her face in Stardust's silky mane, breathing in her sweet pony smell.

"Don't cry," she said gently. "It's not over yet."

"But it is," Stardust wept. "How can we ever escape from here? Divine will destroy the eighth horseshoe and Chevalia will disappear. I'm never going to see my family again." Her voice rose to a wail.

Pippa continued to hug her. She

wanted to say something wise and comforting but the words wouldn't come. At last she pulled away from Stardust to examine the dungeon bars. They ran from floor to ceiling and were as solid as a mountain. They didn't even rattle when Pippa tried to shake them.

"We're truly stuck," she said as Misty came to stand beside her. "Unless . . ." An idea popped into Pippa's head. With mounting excitement she said, "Misty, could you use your unicorn magic to freeze the bars?'"

Misty stared at her for a moment, then a slow smile spread over her face. As Stardust realized what Pippa intended, she stood beside her.

"I think so," said Misty.

As the unicorn bent her head forward, Pippa was amazed by how delicate her spiraled horn looked against the thick prison bar. Could something so tiny and beautiful overpower the iron's strength?

"Yes," Pippa said softly.

She clenched her hands into fists. It was like good and evil. Good always won in the end if people had the courage to stand together and fight the bad.

A cracking noise echoed around the prison cell as, slowly, the bars began to freeze. Pippa could feel the cold radiating from them.

"It's your turn now, Stardust," said Pippa. "Can you kick the bars out?"

Stardust shook back her long, white

mane. There was a look of determination in her brown eyes.

"Easy!" she said.

Turning her back on the bars, Stardust lashed out with her hind hooves
and there was an earsplitting crack.
Stardust kicked again and again. Suddenly the bars fell to the floor.

"Hooray!" cheered Pippa.

She scrambled up on Stardust's back. "Now we go after Divine."

At a fast trot, Stardust and Misty fled the dungeon into the dark tunnel. Many of the flickering torches had been snuffed out. Pippa squinted as they flew along, but the passageway didn't look familiar.

"Left," she said uncertainly as they reached the first branch of the underground labyrinth.

Pippa clung onto Stardust's back, ducking her head in the places where the ceiling was low. Stardust's and Misty's breathing came in noisy rasps. They continued for a while, until they reached a crossroad of four paths. Pippa hesitated.

"Which way?" Stardust asked, pulling up.

Fear gripped Pippa's insides. She didn't remember this part of the tunnel at all. There was a buzzing noise in her ears. Pippa shook her head in irritation.

"Watch out!" cried a tiny voice. "It's meee. Your good friend Zzzimb."

"Zimb!" Pippa's spirits soared as her horsefly friend flew in front of her face and landed on her nose. Pippa giggled and crossed her eyes as she tried to focus on him.

Zimb chuckled too, then flew away to perch on Stardust's ear.

"A little lossssssst, are we? Let Zzzimb help."

There was a faint buzz and suddenly

the tunnel glowed with a thousand pinpricks of light.

"Fireflies!" Pippa said, staring around in delight.

"Weee ssssaw you enter the Volcano," said Zimb. "No Royal Pony has ever ventured here before. Weee guesssssed you might need help."

"Thank you," said Stardust.

Quickly Pippa, Stardust, and Misty told Zimb why they were in the Volcano.

"Baronesssss Divine hassss assembled everyone in the castle courtyard," said Zimb. "Weeee sssssaw her on our way in. Hurry!"

Stardust and Misty galloped through the tunnels, led by Zimb and the light of the fireflies showing them where to go. Together they burst into the castle courtyard. As Stardust pulled up, Pippa gasped.

"Wow!" she exclaimed, her eyes staring at the huge crowd of Night Mares assembled in front of Divine.

No one noticed Pippa, Stardust, Misty, Zimb, and the fireflies join the back of the crowd. All eyes were on Divine, who stood on a platform of black rock as she addressed the crowd. Crowning her head was the eighth golden horseshoe, glinting in the fierce light of the Volcano.

"The time has come. This Midsummer Day will go down in our history, for today marks the start of a wonderful new era for the ponies of the Volcano. We are gathered here to witness the end of the Royal Realm. Nightingale was wrong to have meddled with magic. She never should have created Chevalia and allowed ponies from the human world to come here. I will reverse her mistake. By throwing this horseshoe into the lava,

our volcanic island will return to the way it was. Down with Chevalia! Long live Volcanica!"

A loud cheer resounded from the Night Mares and they stomped their hooves with approval.

Out of the corner of her eye, Pippa saw Nightshade and Eclipse huddled together. Their eyes were huge with worry and they shook their heads in disbelief.

"Only they know the truth," Pippa said softly. "If Divine destroys that horseshoe, she'll destroy the whole island."

Chapter 5

The cheers rose to a crescendo, and with it the courtyard darkened. Pippa stared up. What was the dark shape that was spreading closer, like spilled ink? The Night Mares fell silent. A soft whooshing noise filled the air. It reminded Pippa of wings.

"Cloud!" she exclaimed as the silver-gray princess pony led a flock of flying ponies into the courtyard.

"Mom, Dad! Crystal, Cinders . . ." Stardust's voice was soft with wonder as the entire Royal Court flew into sight and hovered above them.

"I saw you enter the Volcano," said Cloud. "I thought you'd probably need some help."

"And I think I saw you!" Pippa exclaimed, thinking of when they stepped into the Volcano Castle and she'd noticed something in the sky.

Cloud swooped down and rubbed her nose first against Stardust's and then Misty's nose. There was a loud crack and a bright flash of light as they both sprouted wings. Pippa adjusted her position on Stardust's back around the princess pony's new wings.

"You dare to invade my castle?" Divine demanded, her eyes rolling wildly. "What's the meaning of this?"

"We've come to save Chevalia, for the good of all the ponies who live here," Cloud replied.

"Too late!" shrieked Divine.

She tossed her head and the golden horseshoe spun into the air. It flew over the Volcano, spinning in the wind. Then it fell toward the fiery pit of the Volcano.

Pippa shouted to Stardust, "Get it!"

Stardust flew down, her mane and tail flying behind her straighter than arrows. Pippa hung on tightly, gritting her teeth as the hot volcanic air washed over them. Far below she could see the lava glimmering red. The horseshoe spun toward it, flashing in the fiery light.

Stardust flew even faster. Pippa could feel the pony's muscles straining as she dived toward the molten heart of the Volcano far below. Burying her left hand in Stardust's mane to anchor herself, she reached out for the spinning horseshoe. Her fingers touched it, but then the horseshoe spun away. Stardust flew faster still. Pippa reached out again. She was so close. Her wavy hair streamed out behind her and the wind rushed in her ears. Her fingers ached as they reached for the horseshoe and, this time, she caught it. The horseshoe tingled in her hand as magic

coursed through her fingertips. It filled her with warmth, excitement, and hope.

"We did it!" she shouted.

Stardust whinnied with delight and, turning around, she soared upward. She flew over the courtyard and circled it in a lap of victory. Pippa sat tall on her back, proudly holding the horse-shoe in the air for everyone to see.

"Stupid fools! You've ruined every-thing," Divine shrieked with rage.

"No," shouted Stardust. "*You* would have ruined everything, but now Chevalia is safe for us all to live in and enjoy again."

"She's right," Nightshade and Eclipse called out. "The Mistress wanted the island for herself. She doesn't care what happens to us."

The Royal Ponies flying overhead cheered wildly, but the Volcano ponies looked doubtfully between Divine and Stardust, unsure who to believe.

"Nightingale created the horse-shoes and Chevalia for everyone," said

Nightshade. "Why would Divine want to destroy them unless it was for her own gain?"

It was as if the Night Mares had suddenly woken up. Their faces cleared as they understood the truth, and they burst into noisy cheers.

"To Chevalia!"

The applause and cheering lasted for a while. As the noise finally died away, Stardust spoke.

"We haven't succeeded yet. For Chevalia to remain the beautiful place it is, we have to hang this horseshoe on the ancient Whispering Wall by sundown."

Queen Moonshine flew over the center of the courtyard.

"Go quickly, my foal—time is running out. Then tonight we will celebrate, first with a Royal Concert with our new friends the unicorns, then with the Midsummer Ball. Everyone is invited—you are all my guests. From this day forth the Royal Ponies and the Volcano ponies will be better friends. The island of Chevalia belongs to us all."

"Never!" shrieked Divine. "I will never allow it."

The guards surrounded Divine, but she was too quick. Leaping in the air, she threw herself at Queen Moonshine. The queen backed away in alarm, flapping her pale gold wings, but not before Divine had rubbed noses with her.

There was a brilliant flash of light and a crack split the air as the Baroness sprouted her own wings. Whinnying in triumph, Divine flew away.

"Stop her," shouted the guards.

Ponies bolted in all directions, until the queen called them to attention.

"Don't fear Divine. It's unlikely that

she'll show her face around here again. But if she does, we'll be ready for her. If all of us stand together, we can stop her from carrying out any more evil plans."

Pippa leaned forward and spoke into her friend's ear.

"Stardust, we have to go."

"I know," said Stardust. "Hold on tight, Pippa."

The princess pony's white wings flapped gracefully as she rose up and out of the Volcano and headed for home.

Chapter 6

With the sun setting behind her, Stardust flew straight to Stableside Castle. Pippa urged her to fly faster as the sinking sun fell toward the horizon. As Stableside came into view, the sun was merely a golden sliver above the darkening sea. With a burst of energy, Stardust flew over the castle walls and landed in the Royal Courtyard. The moment her hooves touched the ground, her wings disappeared. Pippa had to hold on tightly.

"There's not much time left," Stardust said as she approached the ancient Whispering Wall.

Pippa heard the rush of wings as the entire Royal Court returned behind them. All but Cloud landed in the courtyard—she remained above the ground, keeping her hooves tucked up beneath her.

The last rays of the sun lit the seven golden horseshoes on the wall. The magic crackled as it renewed itself, but Pippa could see the bare patch of wall where the eighth horseshoe needed to be placed.

As Stardust came next to the wall,

Pippa stood up on her back. A smile tugged at her lips as she remembered how scared she'd been the very first time she'd stood on Stardust. That had been to rescue the first golden horseshoe. She'd never completely got rid of her fear of heights but she'd come a long way to manage it. Proudly Pippa reached up and hung the golden horseshoe back where it belonged.

A sunray slanted toward it and, reaching down, kissed the horseshoe with its buttermilk glow. There was a moment of complete silence, then the Whispering Wall seemed to let out an electric sizzle. Suddenly it was as if someone had lit a thousand sparklers. The horseshoes glittered brighter than

the noonday sun as their energy was fully renewed.

A huge cheer rose into the air, along with cries of "Chevalia forever!"

Pippa slid from Stardust's back and threw her arms around her friend's neck.

"We did it," she sobbed. Happiness

filled her like a mountain stream. "We found all the missing horseshoes. We saved Chevalia."

Stardust nuzzled Pippa's hair.

"Thank you, Pippa," she neighed. "And thank you for being my best friend."

As the very last ray of sunlight disappeared, a warm, amber light bathed the whole island. The energized horseshoes were charging the island's magic for another year. Stardust stood very still, drinking it in. All of a sudden, for Pippa, time froze. The courtyard became sketchy like a shadow, and through it she could see her family on the beach in the horseshoe-shaped cove. Her mother, brother, and sister were as still as statues, sitting with a picnic half laid out before them. A wave of longing swept over Pippa. She missed her family so much it hurt.

The light disappeared, leaving Stardust and Pippa in the darkness. Time moved on again.

"I love Chevalia," Pippa said softly, "but I love my own home too. It's time I returned to my family."

"Of course," said Stardust. "You can't leave just yet, though."

Pippa raised an eyebrow, making Stardust giggle.

"You can't miss the Royal Concert or the Midsummer Ball."

There was so little time to prepare for the concert that everyone pitched in and helped. Pippa smiled as Queen Moonshine rushed past her with a huge bunch of wildflowers for King Firestar to hang around the Royal Court.

Just as the last garland was put in place, the unicorns arrived from the Cloud Forest. They were greeted by court advisers who'd hurriedly changed into their best sashes and who ushered all the guests to the courtyard.

The opening bars of music soared in the air and Pippa's heart flew with it as she was carried away by the exquisite voices. Honey's coat looked pale in the moonlight as her duet approached. She needn't have worried. She sang beautifully, her confidence boosted by her unicorn twin and singing partner, Goldie. Afterward Stardust whispered to Pippa that the concert was the best one Chevalia had ever held. Queen Moonshine thought so too.

"Much good has come from these troubled times. The ponies and unicorns who live here on Chevalia need not fear each other anymore. We will work and play together for the good of the island and all ponykind."

"What, even the Night Mares?" called a pony who hadn't flown to the Volcano with the Royal Family.

"Especially the *Volcano ponies*," Queen Moonshine answered. "They're no different than us."

☆

The courtyard was full of nervous neighs, but when the Volcano ponies arrived for the ball, shyly shuffling their hooves, every single pony welcomed them warmly.

Riding on Stardust's back as they danced with Prince Jet and Prince Storm, Pippa was bursting with happiness.

"Ouch!" Stardust squeaked, as Jet stepped on her hoof again.

"Sorry." Jet blushed. "Dancing's not really my thing."

"Look at Crystal and Trojan." Honey giggled, pointing to the other side of the room with a sparkly hoof.

Crystal and Trojan, the farm pony from the Grasslands, were dancing together, nuzzling as they swayed to the music.

"And there's Blossom," Stardust said, her eyes wide with surprise. "Who'd have thought my 'clumsy' friend would be so good at dancing?!"

"It just shows you don't know what you're good at until you try different things," Pippa said, remembering all the new things she'd tried and achieved in the last week.

There was a huge banquet at the ball. Pippa realized how hungry she was as she and Stardust ate from the flower-decorated troughs. Stardust enjoyed honey-dipped carrots

and roasted oats while Pippa polished off a glass of lemonade and a plate of fish and fries prepared especially for her.

☆

Soon the wonderful Midsummer evening was drawing to a close. As the ponies began to drift back to their stables, Princess Cloud flew overhead.

"It's time, Pippa. I'm here to take you home."

Stardust's eyes filled with tears.

"I can hardly bear to let you go," she whinnied.

Cloud looked at her youngest sister.

"Would you like to come with us and fly your friend home?" she asked.

"Yes," Stardust said immediately. "I'd love that."

Cloud flew over to rub Stardust's nose and right away she grew a huge pair of feathery, white wings. Pippa neatly jumped onto her back amid cries of farewell from her new friends.

Queen Moonshine's voice rose above them all.

"Good-bye, Pippa MacDonald, friend of Chevalia. You're always welcome here. Come back and see us soon."

Pippa choked back her tears.

"I will," she said, waving. "Bye, Honey. Bye, Goldie. Bye, Blossom and Misty, Comet, Jet, Crystal, Storm, King Firestar, Peggy, and good-bye, Cinders."

With a dip of their wings, Stardust

and Cloud rose into the moonlit sky and up over the glass-like sea.

"Wait," Pippa cried, seeing two huge horselike forms emerging from the water. "It's Triton and Rosella!"

The giant seahorses bowed their heads as Stardust hovered above them.

"Pippa, lover of ponies, thank you for saving our island," they yelled.

"Thank you for helping me," Pippa yelled back.

A warm glow filled Pippa as Stardust sped away. She was glad she'd seen her seahorse friends one last time. It was with them that the entire adventure on Chevalia had started.

☆

Stardust and Cloud flew side by side in silence. Gradually the dark night gave way to the rosy light of dawn and the sky brightened, until it was blue in the midday sun.

Cloud and Stardust both slowed, their huge wings straining with effort.

"Can you feel it?" asked Cloud. "We've left the magic time bubble behind. You're nearly home, Pippa."

Pippa wrapped her arms around Stardust's soft neck.

"Best friend," she whispered, "I'm going to miss you."

"I'll miss you too," Stardust said, her voice full of tears. "But remember— it's not good-bye. We'll meet again. I know it."

"Me too," said Pippa.

They were hovering just above the sand by the horseshoe-shaped cove. Pippa hugged Stardust one last time and, as she did so, Stardust pressed something cold into Pippa's hand.

"To remember me by," she said softly.

Then Pippa slid from Stardust's back and dropped to the soft sand. The whir of wings overhead faded and, as Pippa stared into the bright blue sky, Cloud and Stardust vanished.

The beach was quiet except for the soft hiss of the sea as it lapped against the shore. Pippa rubbed her eyes.

Suddenly it was hard to imagine she'd been anywhere at all. Had she fallen asleep and had the most amazing dream? Her hand tightened around something solid. She unclenched her fingers and in her palm was Stardust's sparkly pink tiara. Pippa stared at it for a few seconds then carefully slid it into the pocket of her shorts. As she did so, she realized she was back in her own clothes.

"Pippa!"

Mom was calling.

Pippa raced up the beach. Mom was just putting up a parasol over a blanket that was spread with an amazing picnic. The Midsummer Ball now seemed a lifetime ago and she was ravenously hungry. Sitting down between her sister, Miranda, and her brother, Jack, she reached for a sandwich.

"This is going to be the best vacation ever," Pippa declared.

Mom smiled as she handed out cups of juice.

"And that's even before I've told you about my final surprise."

Pippa hurriedly swallowed a mouthful of sandwich.

"What surprise?" she asked.

"I know how much you like ponies—"

"*Love* ponies," Pippa corrected her.

Mom smiled. "Just down the lane from the vacation cottage there's a riding school, and guess what? I've arranged for you to have riding lessons.

Wouldn't you love to learn to ride a pony?"

Pippa was speechless for a moment. Then she jumped up and hugged her mom so hard that she nearly dropped her drink.

"Thanks, Mom. It's a dream come true!"

Chevalia Now!

**EXCLUSIVE
INTERVIEW WITH PIPPA
AND PRINCESS STARDUST**

by Tulip Inkhoof

1

While Chevalia was celebrating the return of the eight magical horseshoes and enjoying the festivities, this dedicated reporter interviewed Princess Stardust and Pippa MacDonald in between the Royal Concert and the Midsummer Ball. ✧ ✧ ✧

☆ **TI (Tulip Inkhoof):** Well, you two are certainly the toast of the party. How does it feel to have saved Chevalia?

☆ **S (Princess Stardust):** It feels incredible!

☆ **P (Pippa):** It does feel great but, Stardust, let's not forget that saving the horseshoes was a team effort. We couldn't have done it by ourselves.

☆ **S:** You're right, Pippa—the entire island came together to help.

2

TI: Yes, and even the Night Mares are here at the castle for the ball?

S: You mean the Volcano ponies, don't you? We used to call them Night Mares but that was an unfair name— we never took the time to get to know them. The Volcano ponies are the original inhabitants of Chevalia, and our very special friends.

P: That's very grown-up of you, Stardust. I think you've learned a lot this week.

TI: My word, have you only been on Chevalia for a week, Pippa?

☆ **P:** Yes, I can't believe it either!

☆ **S:** As soon as I
saw this real, live
girl on the beach
that first morning,

I just knew she'd come to save the island.
What I didn't know was that she'd become
my best friend too!

☆ **P:** I'm going to miss you so much, Stardust.

☆ **S:** Do you really have to go home to the
human world? Can't you stay on Chevalia?

☆ **P:** It's so tempting, but I love my family
and, even though they're not missing me
because of the time bubble, the truth is
that I miss them.

☆ **S:** I understand—I'd miss my family too.

☆ **TI:** What will you do back in the human world, Pippa? It's such a mystery to us Chevalia ponies.

☆ **P:** Well, we'll still be on vacation when I return, which I'm really looking forward to, and soon after that it's back to school.

☆ **S:** Won't you miss the excitement of Chevalia?

☆ **P:** Of course I will, but Chevalia will always be in my heart and in my memories. Besides, everything can be an adventure.

☆ **S:** That's so true—and I hope I have an adventure every single day!

☆ **TI:** Then that will give me a lot to report on!

5

And with that, Stardust tugged Pippa onto the dance floor for the first dance of the Midsummer Ball, leaving this young reporter to reflect on the incredibly eventful week. This was a week in which our beautiful island was saved and the Royal Ponies made friends with the once mysterious, and long misunderstood, Volcano ponies.

☆ Chevalia Now, Chevalia Forever! ☆

Queen Moonshine and **King Firestar**
invite all the ponies on Chevalia
to the **Midsummer Ball**
at Stableside Castle

A Midsummer celebration with dancing
and a delicious banquet

Please welcome the Volcano ponies
as they make their Castle debut

Dress code: wear your best sashes and sparkliest tiaras!

Dear Ponies of Chevalia,

I'm writing this letter on the big wooden table in our vacation cottage, and I plan to give it to Triton and Rosella to deliver before we drive back to Burlington Terrace.

It's hard to believe I've been back with my family for a whole week. In my heart it feels like I haven't left Chevalia at all.

As soon as Stardust and Cloud dropped me off at the beach, I heard Mom calling me for lunch. We had a delicious picnic on the sand with my sister, Miranda, and my little brother, Jack. While we were eating,

I had the most wonderful surprise—Mom told me she was going to treat me to riding lessons! Every day for the past week, I had lessons with an amazing pony called Snowdrop— the pony from my dreams!

Mrs. Woods, the lady who runs the riding school, encouraged us to learn eventing. Together Snowdrop and I tried dressage, cross-country, and showjumping. Snowdrop and I were such a perfect match that Mrs. Woods said I should return to train with Snowdrop during my next school vacation. I do hope Mom agrees! Perhaps I could visit Chevalia too? Please cross your hooves for me!

Now it's time to return to our house, to school, and to normal life . . . I miss you all so much, especially Princess Stardust. To Chevalia!

Your friend,
Pippa MacDonald

Pippa and Stardust's adventures
in Chevalia are only
just beginning!

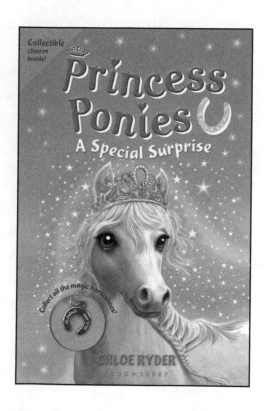

Turn the page to read a sneak peek . . .

"Would you like some more chocolate cake, Pippa?" asked Mom.

Pippa looked at the cake. It was filled with buttercream and topped with chocolate sprinkles, and it tasted delicious. "I'm not sure. If I eat too much then I might be too heavy for Snowdrop to carry me over the jumps tomorrow."

Mom laughed. "Nonsense! Snowdrop's

a big strong horse. She could carry two of you."

Pippa smiled. "I'll have a little slice then, please. I need to keep my strength up. It was hard work jumping Snow-drop today. Did I tell you how we cleared the wall? Mrs. Woods said it was a perfect jump."

Miranda, Pippa's older sister, rolled her eyes. "Yes, but you've only told us about it six times."

"Have I? I'm really excited and nervous about the riding school compe-tition tomorrow. It must be making me forgetful."

Pony-mad Pippa MacDonald was on a seaside vacation with her mom, Miranda, and younger brother Jack.

There were stables nearby and at the start of the vacation, Mom had secretly arranged for Pippa to have riding lessons there as a surprise. The stables had a pony called Snowdrop, named after a famous show pony. Pippa had a poster of the famous pony on her bedroom wall at home, so she was thrilled when she was given Snowdrop to ride.

Pippa had a secret too. On the first day of her vacation, two giant seahorses had whisked her away to Chevalia, a magical island where Royal Ponies reigned. Chevalia had been in danger. Pippa and her princess pony friend, Stardust, had saved the island by finding eight golden horseshoes.

Don't miss Pippa's journey to find the golden horseshoes and save Chevalia!